Peach Cobbler Poison

*The Drunken Pie Café Cozy Mysteries,
Book One*

By Diana DuMont

Chapter One

I grimaced as I glanced at the clock above the door of the Drunken Pie Café. The hour hand was creeping slowly toward the five—closing time—and I still hadn't sold even a tenth of what I'd baked this morning.

What had I been thinking? That I could give up a lucrative legal career in a big city like San Francisco, move to a small town in wine country, and have instant success at opening my own pie shop? It had all sounded so good in theory, but reality was biting me hard right now. My grandma, whom I affectionately called Grams, had tried to warn me that breaking into the business world of Sunshine Springs wouldn't be easy, but I hadn't listened to her. What did an old, quirky lady like her really know about running a small business?

Apparently, she knew more than I'd thought. I'd been convinced that my café concept—a pie shop that sold boozy pies paired with wine—would be the perfect afternoon stop for the fine citizens of this sundrenched little town. But true to Grams' warning, the locals weren't interested in supporting a non-local. And even though my driver's license now boasted a Sunshine Springs address, everyone here still considered me an outsider.

Honestly, I felt like an outsider. But I'd begun to feel like an outsider in San Francisco, too. After I caught my husband cheating on me and filed for divorce, all of our mutual friends had turned their backs on me. They acted as though *I* had somehow been the one that did something wrong. After ten years of marriage, most of our friends had been mutual friends, so I wasn't left with many allies. And after ten years of dreaming of escaping city life, I'd decided that the middle of the divorce was the perfect time to start over.

Who could blame me for feeling that way? I just hoped I hadn't blown all my savings on a café concept that wasn't going to work.

I turned to straighten the stack of coffee mugs on the counter behind me. On Grams' advice, I'd made sure to offer espresso drinks and coffee in addition to wine. After all, some customers might be looking for a shot of caffeine to replenish their energy before heading to one of the big, local wineries for another wine tasting. I offered non-alcoholic pies, too. Gotta keep everyone happy with plenty of options.

But having options hadn't brought in business, and I cursed under my breath at the coffee mugs and wine glasses that had gone unused all day long. Maybe I should admit defeat and just close up for the day. I wasn't likely to get any customers in the last thirty minutes of the café's open hours.

But no sooner had I decided that closing for the day was the best option than the bell above the front door jingled. Startled, I turned around with a big smile on my face. Perhaps the next half-hour wasn't going to be a total waste, after all.

"Good afternoon!" I said with a bit too much peppiness in my voice. But the smile on my face quickly faded when I saw that it was only a delivery man.

"Afternoon," he said, seemingly oblivious to the fact that my smile had suddenly turned into a scowl. "I have a big, huge box for you here. Not sure what it is, but man is it heavy."

"Oh!" I brightened somewhat. "That's probably the wooden sign I ordered for the front of the shop. You can leave it there by the front door. No sense in dragging it all the way to the back when I'm just going to have to drag it back to the front."

"Super. I'll just need a signature, then."

I resisted the urge to roll my eyes. I couldn't believe the little sign company I'd ordered from was requiring a signature, as if there was some sort of huge black market for reselling custom made signs. It wasn't the delivery man's fault, though, so I came around the counter without protest and signed the tablet he held out for me. As he fiddled with the tablet, I started tearing open the box.

"It is my sign!" I exclaimed. The rich wood was painted with vibrant colors that looked even more beautiful than I'd dared to hope. Above the painted slice of pie and wine glass, the words "The Drunken Pie" had been expertly scripted onto the wood.

"Hey, that's not bad," the delivery man said. "It looks a whole lot better than the Main Street Café sign down the road."

I sighed. "Thanks. Not that it's going to help me get any business. I'm not local enough for people to want to buy pie from me."

The delivery man shrugged. "Don't worry. People here try to act like some exclusive club, but they won't be able to resist your pie for long. Not when it smells so good. My mouth started watering before I'd even opened the front door."

I smiled gratefully. "Thanks. I hope you're right."

I had a feeling this guy was just saying that to be nice, but hey—at least he *was* being nice. That was more than I could say for a lot of people around here.

"I'm always right," he said with a wink, then held out his hand. "I'm Scott, by the way. Scott Hughes. I'm responsible for nearly all deliveries in Sunshine Springs, so I'll probably be seeing quite a bit of you."

"Isabelle James," I said as I shook his hand. "I guess you already knew that since I had to sign for the package. But most people call me Izzy."

"Izzy James. Nice name. And nice to meet you."

He gave me a wide smile, and I felt like perhaps I'd made my first friend in this town. The thought made me giddy, and I decided to offer him a complimentary slice of pie. Before I could make the offer, though, the smile disappeared from his face.

"Uh-oh. I gotta go. Here comes trouble."

I frowned, and turned to look in the same direction that he was looking. Two stunning woman who looked almost like twins were walking down the sidewalk arm-in-arm, laughing at something a tall man next to them had just said. The two women were dressed in skirt suits, and the man wore dress slacks and a crisp white shirt. A large camera was slung over his shoulder by an expensive-looking leather strap. The trio wasn't dressed casually like most of the locals in Sunshine Springs, but their clothing didn't look like the overly trendy styles that the wine-country tourists favored, either.

"Trouble?" I asked, glancing over at Scott again. He was already reaching for the front door.

"Yeah, trouble. Those three are journalists from the big city. You know, San Francisco. They came down here to cause trouble for Theo. I'm sure you've heard of him?"

I nodded. Theo Russo owned the Sunshine Springs Winery, and was widely regarded as the richest, handsomest man in town. I stocked his award winning pinot noir in my café, as did pretty much every restaurant in Sunshine Springs. "Are these journalists doing a story on Theo?"

"Yeah, and not a nice one. They're trying to invent some scandal. I ran into them earlier today while making a delivery. They were in the middle of a huge argument with Theo, and of course I took his side. Anyway, I'm out of here. You were my last delivery of the day, and I'm not interested in running into that crew again. I'll see you later. Good luck with the pie."

Before I could reply, Scott ran out the front door, hopped into his delivery truck, and sped away from the café. I watched as the three journalists continued to walk down the street. I saw one of the women point at the delivery truck and say something as it drove away. She crossed her eyes, and her two companions laughed. The man pointed at where the delivery truck had just been, and made a hand gesture that I was pretty sure was meant to indicate that Scott was crazy.

The frown that still stretched across my face deepened as I watched them. What a bunch of brats. They did not look like nice people at all.

And they looked like they were heading straight toward my café.

Chapter Two

My initial assumption proved correct: the three journalists were not nice people. From the moment they walked into my café, they gossiped nonstop about who they hated and why. Theo Russo appeared to be at the top of their list, and I forced myself to bite my tongue.

I barely knew Theo. I wasn't under any obligation to defend him, especially when I was still an outsider myself according to all the Sunshine Springs locals. Not only that, but the gossiping trio also proved to be hungry. They bought an entire pie to split, along with two full bottles of wine. I wasn't about to say anything to offend my best paying customers of the day, even if they were jerks. I had bills to pay, and I doubted Theo was going to pay them for me just because I defended his honor to a bunch of journalists.

Besides, I couldn't help feeling a bit curious as to what the supposed scandal down at the Sunshine Springs Winery was all about. I turned my back to the group and pretended to be cleaning a stack of mugs, but really I was eavesdropping on their conversation.

From the bits and pieces I caught, it soon became clear to me that they weren't all journalists. Only one of the women was. Her name was Caitlin, and she worked for the *San Francisco Scandal*, a popular weekly gossip magazine in the "big city," as everyone here referred to San Francisco. The man, Todd, worked as a photographer for the same magazine. But the other woman, Josie, was actually Caitlin's younger sister who was dating Todd and had tagged along for the plush, wine country assignment.

Caitlin was *not* happy about that. She made several snarky comments to both Josie and Todd about their relationship and how it was interfering with her work on uncovering the scandal. But Todd and Josie made snarky comments right back, and said that Caitlin needed to get over herself and accept their relationship.

"Drama, drama," I whispered to myself as I washed the same coffee mug for the fourth time. I wished the group would quit talking about their own little soap opera and say something about the winery.

A few minutes later, I got my wish. The group finally moved on from their family drama arguments and started talking about Theo. In hushed tones, they discussed the Sunshine Springs Winery. According to Caitlin, rumors were flying that Theo was blackmailing the town's City Council into giving him special favors. She even suspected him of forcing the mayor to embezzle funds for him directly from the city's coffers. They were speaking so quietly that I had to strain hard to hear, but I was catching enough to get the gist of the conversation.

My heart pounded with excitement. I was learning about my first small-town scandal. I didn't know why a gossip rag in San Francisco cared so much about Sunshine Springs. I supposed a wine country scandal was always exciting to those living in the nearby big city. But whatever the case, I felt a little thrill of pleasure at realizing that I was one of the first to know about Theo's alleged wrongdoing.

"The thing is," Caitlin whispered, and I tilted my head toward her so I could hear better. But I never got to hear what "the thing" was. At that moment, the front door to my café opened once more, causing the bells to jingle loudly and Caitlin to shut her mouth.

I turned around, surprised that I was going to have yet another customer in the last few minutes of the day. But before I even saw the two women entering, I knew who it was.

My grandmother, Agnes James. I'd know her laughter from a mile away. She swept into the café, her hair colored a startling hot pink shade that clashed violently with the lime green shift dress she wore. An assortment of large, beaded jewelry hung around her neck, spanning just about every color of the rainbow—if rainbows were comprised of neon colors.

"Grams!" I exclaimed. "What are you doing here? I thought you were going to watch Sprinkles today."

Grams waved her hands at me dismissively. "Oh, but I did watch him. He's had a jolly old time today. I daresay he's settling into Sunshine Springs much better than you are."

"That wouldn't take much," I muttered. "But this morning you insisted on taking him all day so he wouldn't be alone. And now you're out here at the café without him, which means he's alone."

"Not at all, darling. Not at all." Grams shooed away the other woman who had entered with her—an older woman who was one of about twenty of Grams' closest friends. Grams had quite the social life here in Sunshine Springs. As the other woman stepped aside, I saw that my Dalmatian, Sprinkles, had been sitting behind her the whole time.

Sprinkles looked up at me with accusing eyes, as though asking how I could possibly have thought it was a good idea to leave him with Grams all day. He was wearing a hot pink bandana, and even from across the room I could see that his toenails had been painted hot pink as well.

"Grams! What on earth did you do to him? He's covered in pink!"

"Yes, isn't it darling? I took him down to Sophia's Snips Hair Salon and Spa with me. The ladies there all fell in love with him, and one of the nail girls agreed to paint his nails for me. Then I couldn't have his collar not matching his nails, so I bought him a matching bandanna."

"With rhinestones," added the woman standing beside Grams.

I gaped at Grams, and at Sprinkles. I wasn't the only one. From the corner of my eye, I could see that Caitlin and her little crew were gaping as well. They'd fallen silent, and I knew that any chance I had of overhearing any juicy gossip had flown out the window when my grandmother arrived.

With a sigh, I whistled to Sprinkles. "Here boy. I'll give you a slice of key lime pie for putting up with Grams all day. I know it's your favorite. The non-boozy one, though. I don't think dogs need alcoholic pie."

"I need alcoholic pie," Grams declared. She sauntered across the room with Sprinkles warily following behind her. As soon as Grams sat down at one of the tables near the pie case, Sprinkles darted away and came around the corner to me. His doleful eyes told me that I still wasn't quite forgiven, even as I handed him a giant slice of key lime pie.

"What kind of pie would you like, Grams?" I asked. "And do you want coffee or wine?"

"Do you even have to ask? Wine, of course. I'll take a glass of the Sunshine Springs reserve pinot. And I'll try a slice of that peach brandy cobbler."

I noticed that Caitlin looked over and raised an eyebrow at the mention of the Sunshine Springs wine, but I did my best to ignore her. I didn't want to drag Grams into the scandal. At least not yet. As soon as Grams caught wind of it, the whole town was likely to know.

"Just coffee for me, thanks," said the woman Grams had brought in with her. "Decaf, if you don't mind."

I looked at the woman—really looked at her—for the first time since she'd entered the café. She was wearing a plain black dress and shoes that had obviously been chosen for comfort over style. Her hair was white as snow and pulled back into a wispy bun. The only jewelry she had on was a pair of small diamond studs. Her hands shook slightly as she sat down, and I almost asked if she was alright. She was acting so *old*, which made sense. Given the lines on her face and the whiteness of her hair, she must have been about Grams' age. But Grams never acted old. Grams acted more energetic than many twenty-year-olds.

Before I could inquire after the woman's health, though, Grams was introducing her.

"Izzy, this is Violet. She's one of the ladies I play bridge with on Thursdays. I ran into her at the hair salon today and told her she simply must come see your new pie shop. Violet, this is my granddaughter, Izzy."

I told Violet I was pleased to meet her, then hurried to get her some coffee. She looked like she could use a warm beverage. Sprinkles had finished his pie and was looking pitifully at me, his eyes asking for more.

"No, Sprinkles. I don't care how pink your toenails are. You can't have any more pie. You'll get sick!"

"What kind of name is Sprinkles for a boy dog?" Violet asked.

I frowned, suddenly not feeling in as much of a hurry to get her a cup of coffee. "It fits. He's a Dalmatian. He looks like he has chocolate chip sprinkles all over him."

"Sprinkles is a girl name," Violet declared, shaking her head at me.

"Oh, Violet," Grams said. "You have to understand that Sprinkles grew up in San Francisco. The lines between men and women are a bit different there than they are in Sunshine Springs."

"Says the woman who had my *boy* dog's nails painted hot pink," I retorted. Grams grinned at me, but I refused to grin back as I went to get her wine and pie. Grams could drive me a bit crazy sometimes, but I loved her dearly. Despite how much she liked to tease me, I knew she wouldn't hesitate to take out anyone who spoke ill of me with that oversized, neon purple handbag she always carried.

I served Grams and Violet, then busied myself doing the little bit of cleanup that still needed to be done. After spending a few minutes gaping at Grams and Violet, Caitlin had gone back to her own conversation with Todd and Josie. I tried to catch more snippets of what they were saying, but none of it had anything to do with Theo or the winery. They were back to arguing over Todd and Josie's relationship, and I sighed in frustration. Grams had inadvertently ruined my chances at hearing insider information on what was sure to become hot gossip around Sunshine Springs.

Violet quickly downed her coffee, and then nervously looked around as though she somehow wasn't perfectly safe in the middle of a café in this sleepy little town.

"I should get going," she announced as she shakily stood. "It's going to be dark soon."

I frowned. "It's only five, and it's the middle of July. It's not going to be dark for several more hours."

"Still. It's getting late. Better to get home. I'll see you at bridge tomorrow, Agnes."

"See you there," Grams replied, not bothering to argue with Violet about how late it was. As soon as Violet was gone, Grams started talking about her.

"I swear that woman is going to give herself a heart attack one of these days. She thinks every shadow is someone waiting to jump out and kill her. Ever since her husband died—of completely natural causes, mind you—she's been convinced that someone is out to get her. What a sad way to live."

Grams shook her head and took a long swig from her wine glass. Then she whistled and called for Sprinkles. "Here, boy!" she called out. "Come to Grams! I've got pie!"

"Grams, no! He's had too much already! And he definitely doesn't need boozy pie!"

But Grams ignored me. Sprinkles had already made it around the counter and to Grams' table, where he was happily gulping down the last bite of her peach brandy cobbler. Apparently, that was all it took for him to forgive her for the salon trip and hot pink toenails.

"Grams, I don't think he should even be in here," I hissed, feeling annoyed. "It's against health code."

I glanced nervously over at Caitlin's table, hoping that she, Todd and Josie weren't annoyed by the dog. The last thing I needed right now was for some journalist from San Francisco to decide to make trouble for me with Sunshine Springs' health inspectors.

But Caitlin and the others weren't paying any attention to Sprinkles. They were in a heated discussion that was growing awkwardly louder.

"Pfft," Grams said as she scratched Sprinkles behind the ears. "There isn't actually much alcohol in a boozy pie. It gets baked out. And no one here cares about silly health code rules. Why, Alice down at the Morning Brew Café lets her two cats have the complete run of the place. No one complains about that."

"Well, Alice is a local. I'm still an outsider, as you like to remind me. I'm not sure I can get away with all of the things that—"

An angry scream from Caitlin interrupted me. Startled, I looked over to see her jumping to her feet and shaking an angry finger in Todd's face.

"You're wrong. You're both wrong. This relationship is going nowhere. I wouldn't even be working with you if my boss hadn't forced me to. And you, Josie!"

Caitlin turned to point at her sister.

"I'm ashamed to even call you my sister right now. I can't believe you're dumb enough to think this…this…imbecile is actually boyfriend material."

With that, Caitlin grabbed her leather tote bag, spun on her heel, and stormed out of the café. The four of us inside were left to stare after her in stunned silence. Todd was the first to speak. He looked over at me with an embarrassed smile on his face.

"I'm sorry about that outburst. She gets a bit, uh, feisty at times. I hope we didn't disturb your other customer."

He glanced over at Grams, who was still staring out the window with a glint in her eye. She did love a good dramatic moment. I had a feeling she was a bit jealous of Caitlin. Grams probably wished that she had a good reason to storm out of a café like that, with everyone left behind gaping at her in astonishment.

"Don't worry," I assured Todd. "She's my grandmother, so it'll take more than one angry outburst to scare her away from the café. She's sort of stuck with me."

Todd grinned at me, and I had to admit that I couldn't blame Josie for wanting to date him. His tanned skin and chiseled jawbone could have gotten him a career as a male model. I had no idea how good of a photographer he was, but I'd be willing to bet that he'd be even better in front of the camera than behind it.

Another sudden scream rang out across the café, interrupting my brief daydream over Todd's good looks. I snapped my gaze over to Josie, who had jumped from her chair with her hands pressed over her mouth in shock. I followed her gaze, and nearly screamed myself.

Caitlin was lying on the ground in the middle of Main Street. I couldn't be completely sure from this angle, but it looked like the front wheel of a large, white sedan was far too close to Caitlin's skull.

"She's been hit! She's been hit!" Josie shrieked. Tears started running down her face as she ran toward the front door of the café.

"Oh my god!" Todd exclaimed, jumping up to run after her, Grams hot on his heels. Sprinkles was barking, and looking back and forth between the door and me, as if unsure whether to go join the excitement or to stay and protect me from whatever disturbance was causing all of this screaming.

"Come on, Sprinkles," I said as I started running toward the door. I was already pulling my cell phone out of my apron pocket to call 911. "We better see what's going on."

I gave the 911 operator my address and explained that we needed an ambulance, but by the time I hung up the call it was clear that an ambulance wasn't going to do much good.

"She's dead!" Josie wailed. "My sister is dead! And YOU killed her!"

Josie started to rush toward the driver's side of the white sedan, but Todd grabbed her and pulled her back. "Calm down, Josie," he said. "This was an accident, and the ambulance will be here soon."

I turned to look at the driver of the vehicle, and my eyes widened when I saw that Violet was sitting behind the wheel. Her hands were covering her mouth and shaking violently, and she had tears running down her face.

"I didn't see her!" Violet cried. "I didn't see her at all. She just came out of nowhere and threw herself into the street. Why would she do that?"

"Shh, it's alright," Grams said, patting Violet in a rather desperate way, like a frazzled mother might pat a newborn who refuses to sleep more than five minutes at a time. "I'm sure the ambulance will be here soon. I already hear the sirens."

I could hear the sirens too, which was surprising since they were nearly drowned out by Josie's screams and Sprinkles' barking. But a few minutes later, the ambulance came barreling down Main Street and screeched to a halt in front of the Drunken Pie Café. All up and down the street, I could see bystanders peering at the scene, a mixture of genuine horror and brazen curiosity evident in their facial expressions.

The paramedics rushed to Caitlin's side, but it was no use. It only took a few moments for them to look up and shake their heads.

"Dead on arrival," one of them said somberly.

At his words, Josie screamed and fainted into Todd's arms. A split-second later, I looked over to see Violet fainting as well, toppling sideways out of the car and landing in Grams' arms.

All up and down the street, the gawkers were still watching. A few of them were even taking out their phones to take pictures of the scene. I felt disgusted at their crassness, and I hoped they didn't realize that the woman on the ground was actually dead. Taking pictures of a dead woman surely surpassed the boundaries of even the most gossip-hungry among them.

I gave Grams a helpless look as she passed off the unconscious Violet to one of the paramedics.

"Are you okay?" I asked weakly, although I wasn't sure what I would do for her if she wasn't. I didn't exactly feel like a pillar of calm strength myself at the moment. Thankfully, Grams didn't seem too disturbed by the whole affair. She merely shook her head sorrowfully, looking back and forth between Caitlin's lifeless body and Violet's unconscious form.

"Pity," she said. "This ordeal isn't going to do any favors for Violet's nerves. She'll probably have to double the doses on all her anxiety medication."

For a moment, we both were silent. Even Sprinkles had settled down now, having realized that his barking to sound the alarm was no longer necessary. After a few seconds of silence, Grams brightened and turned to me.

"On the plus side, though, this girl's death will be a boon for you."

I raised my eyebrows, a bit shocked. "What on earth do you mean by that?"

Grams winked at me. "Oh, trust me. Everyone's going to want the gossip about this little accident. And they're going to come directly to the scene to get it. Your days of slow sales at the Drunken Pie Café are over."

Grams looked so gleeful that I felt a bit embarrassed for her. "Grams, listen to yourself! Someone just died! The last thing anyone should be worried about right now is pie sales."

Grams raised her hands in a gesture of surrender. "I'm just saying!"

She winked at me, then turned to speak to the paramedics, who were asking her if she knew whether Violet was on any medication.

"Oh, tons," Grams said, and began to list them off.

I stood uncomfortably on the sidewalk, not sure whether reaching out to offer condolences to Josie and Todd would be appropriate or helpful at the moment. So instead, I turned to look at Sprinkles, who was desperately scratching at his hot pink bandana in an attempt to get it off. It's like he knew the whole town was watching him right now, and he wanted to be sure they knew that he was not, in fact, a hot pink and rhinestones kind of guy.

"They're all watching us, Sprinkles," I murmured. "I think they'll be watching us for the next few days or weeks. And I'm not sure that's such a good thing."

Sprinkles gave me an understanding sigh, then lay down at my feat in defeat, the sparkling pink bandana still tied firmly around his neck.

Chapter Three

Grams hadn't been kidding when she said the pie shop would be busy. The next day, the line for pies, wine and gossip stretched out my front door and spilled over onto Main Street. It started even before the shop opened. When I arrived in the morning to bake pies, there were already a few people waiting outside the front door even though I didn't open for several more hours. By the time I actually opened, the line was at least twenty people deep. It never slowed down, and I sold completely out of pie by noon.

That didn't stop people from coming in, anyway. I brewed pot after pot of coffee, and went through dozens of bottles of wine. I found myself looking up at the clock once again as it approached closing time, but today my reasons for looking forward to closing were different. I was exhausted, not bored. I thought that the lines would have slowed down as people realized that I didn't have much to tell them about yesterday's accident. But even though the information I had to give was meager, the good folks of Sunshine Springs hung on every word I said. As closing time approached, I felt relieved that I wouldn't have to repeat the same story for what felt like the millionth time.

The shop was finally clearing out, and I decided to start cleaning up. A mountain of dishes stood in the industrial sink behind me, and I wasn't sure whether there was a clean mug left in the building. My bones ached, but my heart was happy. Today's profits would give my savings a good boost—a boost I desperately needed. It didn't matter how well I had planned things. Opening this café had turned out to be much more expensive than I'd thought it would be.

As I walked toward the front door to lock it, I saw a woman standing below my wooden Drunken Pie sign with one hand on her hip. She gazed up at the sign with a furrowed eyebrow, and I wasn't sure whether her expression was one of disgust or delight. As I watched, she dug into her shiny red purse to pull out her cell phone. The next thing I knew, she had turned around and was holding the phone in front of her face. She pointed it at an upward angle so that she could take a selfie of herself with the sign.

I had to laugh. Yesterday, everyone in town would have been embarrassed to be caught in my pie shop. But today, people were taking selfies of themselves in front of my sign.

The woman took a few shots with her phone's camera, and then started scrolling through them. No doubt, she was looking for the best one so that she could post it online and show all of her friends that she'd been at the now-infamous Drunken Pie Café: the café in front of which a journalist from the big city had met her demise just the day before.

The woman looked up, and saw me staring at her. I would have thought she'd be a bit embarrassed to be caught taking selfies with my sign, but she merely shrugged and gave me a grin.

"What can I say?" she asked. "I take selfies with everything around here. I would be remiss if I didn't take one in front of the hottest café in town."

I raised an eyebrow at her. I wasn't sure that I would call my café the hottest café in town. It was popular for today, but that popularity wasn't likely to last once the excitement of someone dying in front of the café faded away. Still, I was enjoying the business while it lasted, and there was something irresistible about the twinkle in this woman's eyes.

"Well, I'm glad you like my sign. Goodness knows I spent enough money on that thing. Who knew custom signs could be so pricey?"

Her smile widened. "It's an adorable sign. I say it was worth every penny. I'm Molly, by the way. I've been looking forward to getting down here and seeing your pie shop all day. I work at the library, so I hear a lot of the town gossip. Your pie shop is all anyone has been talking about today."

I sighed. "I'm Isabelle, but everyone calls me Izzy. It's nice to meet you, although I do wish people were talking about how good my pie is instead of how someone died in front of my pie shop."

"Well, how good *is* your pie?" Molly asked. "If you're still open, I'd love to come in and try a slice. I have to admit that wine and pie are two of my favorite things, so combining the two sounds like a dream come true."

I grinned. "You seem like my kind of gal. Come on in, and I'll get you a glass of wine and some pie. I'm actually sold out of everything, but I did save a slice of banana cream pie for my Dalmatian. You can have it, and Sprinkles will just have to be happy with his regular old dog food tonight."

Molly's eyes widened. "Oh, I wouldn't want to steal pie from your dog. I love dogs, and I wouldn't want to get off on the wrong foot with Sprinkles."

"Don't worry," I called over my shoulder as I walked back into the café and toward the back room. "Sprinkles gets far more pie than he should, anyway. Just sneak him a bite the next time you come in, and I'm sure he'll be perfectly happy to forgive you."

Sprinkles, who had been sleeping in the back room, must have heard me talking about him. He came bounding out into the café, even though I'd told him a thousand times already to stay in the back. I sighed. I hoped that Grams was right, and that people here really didn't care about things like what the health inspector would say about having a dog in a café.

If Molly's reaction to Sprinkles was any indication, then I had nothing to worry about. Molly squealed, crouched down, and stretched out her arms to Sprinkles as though they had known each other their whole lives.

"Sprinkles! It's so nice to meet you!"

I shook my head, amazed at how everyone in the world seemed to automatically love a spotted dog. Then I turned to go get Molly her pie. A few minutes later, Molly was munching on the slice of banana cream pie, and moaning happily as though this was the first time in her life that she'd ever had the pleasure of tasting sugar.

I smiled. "So you like it?"

"Like it? I love it! I can't believe I've lived my whole life until now without trying your pie. This is definitely going to be my biggest, newest vice. Don't you worry, honey. This pie shop is going to do just fine in Sunshine Springs. People here love wine, and they love baked goods. Combining the two is a sure winner. And now that they've tasted your pie, they won't be able to stay away—no matter how much they want to act like they're too cool for outsiders. How much do I owe you?"

I waved my hand dismissively. "Don't worry about it. I wasn't planning to sell that slice anyway, and it's nice to have someone treating me like a friend instead of an alien."

Molly laughed. "Don't worry. Really. Folks around here aren't as bad as they seem at first. They're just a bit wary of anyone coming up from the big city. We've had a few jerks over the years come in, wanting to buy up local property and turn this place into some kind of wine country getaway for all the snobby people from San Francisco. But you're different. You actually want to live here and make your home here. They'll see that soon enough, especially since your grandma is here. She's a town favorite."

I raised an eyebrow. "Really? I wasn't sure. Obviously, I love her to pieces. But she's so…different."

"Everyone around here is different, once you get to know them. It's what keeps life in a small town interesting."

I shrugged. "I guess I never realized how many characters there were around here. I've only visited a few times, for very short visits. Grams always preferred to come visit me up in San Francisco. She liked to get away to the big city and gawk at all the big city folks, as if they were somehow more eccentric than she is."

Molly just laughed and took another bite of her pie.

"Speaking of interesting," I said. "Aren't you going to ask me about the accident yesterday? After all, that's why everyone is coming by here today."

Molly looked up at me and tilted her head sideways in a quizzical way. "I guess that depends. If I ask you about it, do you have anything new to tell me? So far, I've heard that the poor girl tripped on the curb after leaving your café in the midst of an angry argument with her sister and her sister's boyfriend. And she just so happened to be unlucky enough to trip in front of Violet Murphy, who insists on driving that tank of a car even though she shouldn't be driving at all anymore. Of course, Violet didn't see the girl or didn't stop in time, and now that poor girl's skull is embedded with skid marks from the sedan's tires. That about sum it up?"

I laughed. "Yup. That about sums it up. Oh, gosh. I shouldn't be laughing. You must think I'm a horrible person. It's just that after repeating the same story about a thousand times today, it seems to lose some of its horror. It almost doesn't seem real anymore."

Molly smiled kindly at me. "Don't worry. I understand."
Then, she gasped and clapped her hand over her mouth. Alarmed, I
asked her what was wrong.

"Oh dear!" she answered. "I completely forgot to take a selfie
with my pie before I started eating it. Better late than never, I guess."

She dug in her purse for her phone, and once again held it
out to take a selfie, this time with her half-eaten slice of pie.

"You really do like taking selfies, huh?" I asked.

Molly looked a bit guilty. "Yes. I guess I'm a bit old to be so
obsessed with such shenanigans. But I just like to document
everything. Who can blame me? Life is filled with so many moments
of unexpected little pleasures. I'm not rich, but I find joy where I
can."

"Wow. I think that's the most philosophical attitude toward a
selfie that I've ever heard."

Molly beamed as though I'd just awarded her a gold medal. I
beamed back at her. Something about her just made her easy to talk
to. She seemed genuinely nice, and she looked to be about my age. I
had a feeling she might be the first good friend I made in Sunshine
Springs. And really, it only took one insider friend, right? Once I was
in with one person here, I'd be in with everyone. I would no longer
be an outsider. The thought gave me the courage to ask a question
I'd wanted to ask of just about everyone who came in today, but
hadn't dared.

"Speaking of rich, what can you tell me about Theo Russo?"

Molly's eyes darkened somewhat. She pushed a small piece of
pie around her plate with her fork before answering, as though
carefully considering her words. "Theo's alright. I went to high
school with him, actually."

My eyes widened. "You did?"

"Yeah. He was a year ahead of me, and all the girls had huge
crushes on him, myself included. Of course, he was never interested
in a mousy bookworm like me."

"Mousy? You don't look mousy to me."

It was the truth. In fact, Molly looked quite glamorous. She
was dressed in a bright, colorful sundress, and her hair was pulled up
into a tight but fashionable bun. Loose tendrils of her hair had
escaped from the bun, nicely framing her face. Her makeup was done
to perfection. Not too much, not too little. It accented her features
well and brought out the deep blue of her eyes.

Standing across from her, I was the one who felt mousy. After working all day, my hair was anything but neat, and I didn't have a speck of makeup left on my face. Still, Molly was shaking her head.

"Oh, I guess I'm not as mousy as I once was. But back in high school I'm sure I fit the nerd stereotype perfectly. Still, that didn't stop me from daydreaming about winning Theo's heart. Those dreams were eventually crushed by reality, of course. And I have to admit that I'm rather glad about that. Theo is smart and rich, but can act like a jerk sometimes. He's got a bit of a haughty streak."

I looked around my now empty café, as though worried someone might be listening in on my conversation. There was no one around, of course, but I lowered my voice anyway.

"Have you heard the rumors about him? The girl who died yesterday was here to investigate rumors that Theo was blackmailing the Sunshine Springs government and stealing money from them."

I'm not sure how I expected Molly to react. I probably expected her to be shocked. But she merely lifted her shoulder in the slightest of shrugs before shoving another bite of pie into her mouth. After slowly chewing and swallowing, she shook her head.

"I don't buy it. I've heard those rumors, but I don't think there's any truth to them. Theo might act like a jerk sometimes, but he's not a criminal. I just can't believe that he would steal from the government, especially when he has so much money already. Besides, his dad was so upstanding and moral. I remember hearing about how Theo had to endure long lectures from his old man on the importance of being honest."

I frowned. "But high school was a little while ago, no? How long has Theo been in charge of the winery? People change, you know."

Molly frowned. "Well, it has been about ten years since Theo's dad died and Theo took over the winery completely. But I just can't see him doing something like stealing from the town government—though goodness knows that I would love to see him arrested for something. He's so full of pride that it would do him some good to be taken down a few notches."

Molly laughed, as though just the idea of Theo taking a hit to his pride gave her great delight. But before I could make another comment about how you never knew about people's character, the bell above the café's front door jingled. My heart sank as I realized that it was now past five and I had forgotten to actually lock the door. I looked up to tell my newest customer that I was closed for the day and sold out of everything. But the words stuck in my throat when I saw a group of three stern-looking policemen standing in my café.

"Isabelle James?" one of the officers asked.

I didn't like the tone of his voice. It made something in my stomach clench up nervously.

"Yes, that's me." I eyed him warily.

"You need to come with us down to the station."

"What for?"

"We need to take a statement from you, and you might be in a whole lot of trouble."

I stared at the officer, trying to process what he'd just said. He looked quite gleeful when he told me that I might be in trouble.

"What in the world is this about?" I demanded. "Am I under arrest for something?"

The officer sneered. "You will be, if you don't come willingly."

Molly had turned around in her seat, her hand on Sprinkles' head. Sprinkles was growling, but Molly's soft touch seemed to calm him.

"What's this all about?" Molly asked. "This is no way to welcome our newest town member!"

The officer sneered again. "I'm not sure our newest town member deserves a warm welcome. That death in front of her café yesterday? Turns out it wasn't an accident."

Chapter Four

I followed the officer into the station quietly. Turns out he was the sheriff. He introduced himself to me as Sheriff Mitchell, but all the other officers just called him Mitch.

Mitch was anything but quiet. He laughed boisterously, cracked his knuckles constantly, and generally acted as obnoxious as humanly possible. That was probably a good thing, because he was the handsomest police officer I'd ever met. He had that sort of rugged and handsome look that made you think he would be better off being a police officer in the wilds of Montana than in a little old wine country town.

But his good looks were overshadowed by his horrible attitude, and even if I *had* had any sort of interest in him, it wouldn't have mattered. I didn't want to date someone who acted like a jerk. I'd already spent enough of my life in a relationship with someone who was a bit too full of himself. Never again.

After we entered the station, Mitch left me in the front reception area to await my fate alone. I sat there for a long time, wondering if I was really in trouble. I had experience as a lawyer, but only as a contracts lawyer. If I was actually going to be accused of murder, then I needed to get a criminal lawyer. My mind couldn't process everything that was going on. It was impossible that I was being accused of murder, wasn't it? Surely, I had misunderstood something. This must all be a mistake. For one thing, I had seen with my own eyes as Caitlin lay under the wheel of Violet's sedan in the middle of the street. Surely, no one would blame me for that! The whole thing was just a horrible accident. It's not like I had held a gun to Violet's head and told her to run over Caitlin.

Rationalizing everything that was going on didn't help calm the uneasiness in the pit of my stomach. Sitting there alone for what felt like hours didn't help either. In reality, I had probably only been alone about fifteen minutes when the front door of the station opened. To my great relief, in stepped Scott, the delivery guy. I didn't know him very well, and I had no reason to think that he would defend me in this situation. But still, he had been a friendly face yesterday, and I was clinging to any bit of friendliness that I could. Molly had actually offered to come with me down to the station, which was kind of her since she'd only known me for all of about thirty minutes. It's not like she knew me well enough to trust that I wasn't a murderer, if I truly was being accused of murder.

But I had declined her offer, asking her to instead take Sprinkles to Grams and tell Grams what was going on. I hated to upset Grams, and I knew she would be quite upset when she learned I was at the police station. But I had a feeling I was going to need help getting out of this, and Grams was the best one to help me.

Scott raised an eyebrow when he saw me. He set down the box he was carrying with a heavy thump, dusted his hands off on his khaki pants, and gave me an appraising look.

"Don't tell me that you're mixed up in all of this," he said. "Although, I suppose it makes sense, since the girl died right in front of your store."

"But it was an accident," I protested. "Everyone saw what happened. She fell, and got run over."

Scott looked around the room suspiciously, as though making sure that no one else was there. Then he took a step closer to me, leaned in, and spoke in a low voice. "I overheard Mitch talking with one of his officers down at the Morning Brew Café when I was making a delivery there this morning. Apparently, the autopsy report came back and showed that Caitlin had already been dead at the time Violet ran into her."

I blinked in confusion. "But that's impossible. She had just walked out of the café, and trust me, she was very much alive. She was screaming at the top of her lungs because she was so angry at her sister for dating that photographer."

Scott looked around uneasily again, then turned back to me. "Well, the autopsy report showed that the actual cause of death was poison. It must have been a horrible coincidence, but it sounds like what happened was not that Caitlin tripped. She was overcome by poison, fell into the street dead, and Violet happened to be driving down the street at that exact moment. Of course, when Violet ran into her, it appeared at first glance that the obvious cause of death was the head trauma from the car. But that wasn't it at all."

My jaw fell open at Scott's words. Everything suddenly made perfect sense. If Caitlin had died of poison, of course the sheriff would call me down here to the station. I would be a top suspect, since she'd been eating food and drinking wine from my café right before she died. A cold chill ran through me.

"But I'm sure there was nothing poisonous in my pies. Maybe someone dumped something into her drink. One of the other two sitting with her. Goodness knows they were angry enough at her."

Scott looked around uneasily again, then lowered his voice so low that I almost couldn't make out what he was saying. "Look, you seem like a nice person. And you definitely don't seem like the type that would murder someone, especially someone you don't know. I'm sure this will all be cleared up quickly. But it's going to be hard to convince the sheriff that the victim's own sister killed her. Just be careful what you say, and maybe get a lawyer. The judges here aren't nice to outsiders. Luckily for you, the girl's sister and the sister's boyfriend are also outsiders. It's an equal playing field, if you know what I mean."

I groaned. "Great. It's an equal playing field, because everyone here will hate all three of us just as much. They'll be just as happy to pin the murder on any of us to whom it will stick."

Scott looked genuinely distressed at my words, but before he could say anything else, the loud sound of Sheriff Mitchell's voice reached my ears from somewhere down the hallway.

"Uh-oh," Scott said, quickly pushing the package he'd brought toward the front desk of the reception area. The receptionist's desk was empty, which wasn't surprising since it was almost six o'clock at this point. The receptionist probably went home at five. Sunshine Springs didn't seem like the sort of place that had a whole lot of crime, so I doubted the staff here worked much overtime.

"I have to run," Scott said. "Mitch will kill me if he knows what I told you. He wants to be the one to break the shocking news to all of you."

"I swear, I won't tell him that I know or that you told me."

24

"Thank you," Scott said gratefully. "And I'll keep my ears open for you. If I hear anything around town about what might have happened, I'll be sure to let you know."

Before I could thank Scott, Mitch appeared in the room. His face turned purple with anger when he saw Scott.

"Get out of here!" Mitch yelled at Scott. "This here is a murder investigation. It's not a circus open to everyone in town who wants to gossip."

"Sorry," Scott said as he backed away toward the door. "I was just dropping off a package. I'll be going now."

Before Mitch had time to reply, Scott had disappeared through the front door. But the door didn't immediately close behind him. As Scott walked out, Grams walked in. She looked angry, and Violet was with her. Violet held shakily onto Grams' arm, grasping the bright purple fabric of Grams' shirt as though letting go might cause her to slip straight through the floor.

I didn't care how angry Grams was. I had never been so happy to see her and her ridiculous hot pink hair.

"Grams! I'm so glad you're here. There's been some sort of terrible misunderstanding."

"Molly told me," Grams said. "I was over at Violet's house, trying to comfort her after that horrible ordeal yesterday. Molly called and told me that you'd been asked to come to the police station. She said I'd better get down here right away, and then a cop stopped by and told Violet she had to come in, too." Grams turned to look at Mitch. "What is the meaning of this?"

A haughty smile spread across Mitch's face. "Agnes," he said, putting on an air of great, gentlemanly authority. "I'm sorry to tell you that your granddaughter here is suspected of murder. I'll need to get a statement from her, at the least. It's good that you're here with Violet, because I'll need to get a statement from Violet, too."

Violet's eyes widened at the Sheriff's words, and her shaking increased. "A statement?" she asked in a trembling voice. "But I already gave a statement yesterday. I just want to put this behind me!"

"I understand, Violet," the sheriff said. "And I understand that this whole situation has been stressful for you. But I hope you'll feel better knowing at least that you were not responsible for Caitlin's death. She was already dead before you ran into her."

Sheriff Mitch looked at me when he said these words. I knew he was hoping for a big reaction, and even though I'd promised Scott not to tell Mitch that I already knew about the poison, I wasn't going to give Mitch the satisfaction of thinking he'd shocked me when he hadn't. So I remained silent and gave him a stubborn look.

That turned out to be a mistake, though. Mitch's haughty grin widened.

"I see that news doesn't shock you very much, Isabelle. But I suppose it wouldn't, if you're the one who murdered Caitlin."

I started to protest, but before I could say anything much, Grams interrupted.

"Enough with the games, Mitch. If you have some accusations to make, then make them so that my granddaughter can answer properly. I'm sure there's an explanation for all of this. Izzy would never murder anyone. And really, is it necessary to have Violet here? She's already been through so much, and her nerves are shot. She's liable to have a heart attack! If she does, that's on your conscience!"

Mitch looked slightly chastised. Only slightly, but I supposed that was better than nothing.

"I understand. Violet, please don't worry. One of the officers will explain everything, get a quick statement from you, and then you can go home to rest. But as for you, Isabelle, I'm not sure you'll be going home for quite some time."

I resisted the juvenile urge to stick my tongue out at him, and instead followed him, along with Grams and Violet, toward the back of the police station. I wasn't sure where we were going. I hoped it wasn't a jail cell, but either way, being in the bowels of the station wasn't a good feeling.

Actually, I was quite surprised at how large the police station was. For a small town like Sunshine Springs that had supposedly very little crime, they sure needed an awfully big police station. Looking at Mitch, though, I shouldn't have been that surprised. He seemed like the kind of guy who needed a big old police station to make him feel good about himself. Size matters and all that mumbo-jumbo guys like him always bought into.

Thankfully, when we finally stopped walking we weren't at a jail cell. We were at some sort of interrogation room that didn't look very cheerful, but anything was more cheerful than a jail cell.

To my surprise, when Mitch opened the door wider, I saw that Josie and Todd were already there. They were holding hands, and were flanked on either side by two of Mitch's police officers. They eyed me warily as I walked in, and I looked away. I'm sure anything I tried to say to them would only make matters worse.

As soon as we sat down, Mitch stood facing all of us. He proudly crossed his arms in front of him as though he were a school principal and had just caught the lot of us stealing extra Jell-O from the school cafeteria.

"Thank you all for joining me here this evening," he began. "As though you had any choice."

He laughed as if his poor attempt at a joke had been truly funny. I scowled at him, but he either didn't notice or didn't care. He looked sympathetically at Violet as he continued.

"Violet, I think you'll be happy to know that we've discovered that you were not the cause of Caitlin's death. The autopsy report came back today, and it turns out that she was poisoned."

Apparently, this was the first time that Josie and Todd were learning of this. Their eyes widened, and they looked at each other in astonishment. Then they both started talking at once. They demanded that Mitch explain himself, and he was all too happy to do so. He didn't say anything that Scott hadn't already told me, although he was much wordier about saying it than Scott had been.

The bottom line was that Caitlin's death looked suspiciously like a murder, and Mitch suspected that someone in the room had committed the murder. I didn't think I should be one of the top suspects. When you stopped to think about it, I had no motive. I opened my mouth to say that, but before I could get any words out, Mitch was pointing his finger at Todd, Josie, and me.

"All three of you," he said with great flourish, "Are now officially under arrest for the murder of Caitlin Dixon."

The others shrieked, Grams started yelling, and Violet looked like she might faint again. But the only reaction I could manage was a gaping jaw.

This had not been the welcome to Sunshine Springs that I'd been hoping for.

Chapter Five

Grams stood to her feet and slammed her fist on the table. My heart leapt. I knew Grams was going to stick up for me! Even Mitch looked frightened for a moment.

But when Grams spoke, it wasn't me she was worried about.

"Mitch, this is ridiculous. Violet has already been through so much, and now you're putting her in the middle of this hyper-sensationalized murder investigation. If you need a statement from her, fine. Get a statement. But do it away from this circus, and then let her go home."

To his credit, Mitch looked sufficiently chastened. "I suppose you're right, Agnes."

He motioned to one of his officers. "Smith, take Violet out front where it's more comfortable. Get a quick statement from her on what happened and what she remembers, and then let her go home."

Smith nodded and stood, and Grams stood to help Violet.

"Wait a minute!" I said. "Grams, aren't you going to stay and help me?"

Grams waved her hand, as though my being accused of murder was nothing more bothersome than a fly buzzing around her face.

"You'll be fine, Izzy. I know you didn't do it, so you don't have anything to worry about."

And with that, she disappeared into the hallway, leaving me staring after her in shock. Of course I hadn't done anything, and I was glad that my grandmother believed that. But didn't she know that people were wrongly accused of murder all the time! What if I ended up in jail for the rest of my life? I put my head in my hands. Moving to Sunshine Springs seemed like it had been the worst decision of my life. I should've listened to my friend Betsy back in San Francisco, one of the few who had stood by me while my marriage was falling apart. She'd told me that the middle of a divorce was a bad time to make any big life changes, but I hadn't listened. I'd told her that I'd been thinking of the pie shop for a long time anyway, so it wasn't really all that sudden of a decision. But now, I was wishing that I had stayed at my boring lawyer job, reviewing contracts that made me want to cry from how tedious they were.

Too late now.

Mitch was looking at me with a gleeful expression. "Nice that your grandmother is so supportive of you. But that doesn't change the fact that you're a prime suspect, and there's a lot of evidence against you."

"What evidence?" I asked angrily. "So Caitlin ate at my café. That doesn't prove anything. She ate the exact same thing that Josie and Todd ate. If it was poisoned, then why aren't they dead, too?"

Mitch wasn't going to be put off that easily. "Perhaps you slipped poison into just her slice of pie, or just into her drink. Just because they had the same kind of pie doesn't mean you didn't have an opportunity to poison it."

"No, you're wrong. They ordered a full pie, and a full bottle of wine. I didn't choose which piece each one of them ate. They cut up the pie themselves. And they all drank from the same bottle of wine that they poured out themselves. Go ahead. Ask them."

Mitch looked at Josie and Todd. "Is that true?"

I held my breath, half expecting them to lie. After all, anything they could do to throw suspicion on me was a good thing for me. But I guess Josie wasn't thinking that way, thankfully for me.

She nodded sadly. "That's right. We all ate from the same pie and same wine bottle. It's pretty obvious the poison didn't come from that food, but then where did it come from?"

"You idiot!" Todd said.

Josie looked at him in surprise, not seeming to understand that she had just given testimony that strongly acquitted me.

I was happy, of course. But now, my own suspicions were veering toward Todd. Why was he so upset that Josie had told the truth? Did that mean that he was trying to hide something?

Mitch frowned. "Well, there still might have been a way for you to poison just one part of the pie and make sure that Caitlin was the one who ate that portion."

I gawked at him. Was he serious? He clearly wanted to pin this on me, even when the evidence suggested otherwise.

"That's right!" Josie said, seeing a chance to redeem herself in Todd's eyes. "And if I remember correctly, she was strangely trying to position the pie a certain way when she set it down at our table. She must have been trying to position it so that the poisoned part was in front of Caitlin."

I groaned. I *had* been positioning the pie a certain way. I'd been trying to present it at the most attractive angle to some of my few customers of the day.

Mitch was starting to turn slightly purple again. I think he knew he was losing control of this little investigation. "Listen, all of you are under suspicion, and all of you are under arrest. You all were there, and you all had contact with the pie and the wine. That means that it had to be one of you who killed Caitlin. The judge and jury can decide who's telling the truth and who's not."

"Wait a minute," I said. "How do you even know that the pie and wine were what was poisoned? You have no proof of that. Caitlin could have had something to eat or drink before coming into the pie shop that poisoned her. In fact, that seems a lot more likely to me. She hadn't been eating the pie for all that long, so it would've had to have been some strong, quick-working poison for her to die that quickly."

"That's right!" Todd said, happy to grab a hold of any little shred of information that might clear his name. Never mind the fact that if it wasn't the pie, it could easily have been something he'd given to her himself over the course of the day. I was assuming they'd been together all day researching the winery. Mitch must have realized this too, because he only rolled his eyes at Todd.

"All three of you are under arrest, and that's not changing tonight. Isabelle, it was the pie you baked or the wine you sold that killed Caitlin. Josie and Todd, you had the opportunity to put poison in Caitlin's drink or food. Besides, witnesses say that you were having a huge argument right before Caitlin died. Clearly, there was some bad blood between the three of you."

"That's ridiculous!" Josie said. "Caitlin didn't agree with the fact that I was dating Todd, but so what? Older sisters never think anyone is good enough for their younger sisters. I know that. I wouldn't have killed her just because she didn't like my choice of boyfriend!"

"Will you shut up?" Todd exclaimed. Josie gave him a hurt look, but he didn't back down. "Just keep your mouth shut. You're not supposed to say anything until a lawyer comes."

He was right about that, at least. I had already said too much. I knew that Mitch had been carefully noting everything we said, figuring out as he listened how he was going to use it in the case against us. But he had made me so mad that I hadn't been able to completely keep my mouth shut. As far as Mitch was concerned, it didn't matter whether he hung one, two, or all three of us. He just wanted to pin this on an outsider.

Well, he might pin it on an outsider, but that outsider wasn't going to be me. For one thing, I was determined to become a local in Sunshine Springs, not an outsider. And for another thing, I was innocent.

Now, I was just going to have to figure out how to prove that. And that meant that I was going to have to figure out who really killed Caitlin Dixon.

Chapter Six

Three hours later, I had posted bail and was finally walking out the front entrance of the police station. Josie and Todd had posted bail and were leaving as well, but I didn't want to even look at them right now. I was convinced that one of them was responsible for Caitlin's death—probably Todd—and I was angry that my life was being disrupted because of their crimes. If I were a better detective, I would have used the opportunity of walking out of the police station with them to ask questions and try to get some sort of lead on how to prove that they were the guilty ones. But right then, I was too exhausted to be a detective. I was too exhausted to do anything other than see red from anger.

But my anger faded quickly when a horn honking caused me to look in the direction of a little red sports car. In the front seat of that sports car, Sprinkles sat next to Molly.

"Hey, over here," Molly yelled.

As soon as Sprinkles saw me, he barked and jumped right over Molly's lap. He catapulted through her open driver's side window and ran toward me at full speed. I had never been so happy to see my sweet dog as I was right then. This trumped even the night that I'd found out my ex-husband was cheating on me, and Sprinkles had cuddled next to me in bed all night. I didn't know what I would do without that dog and his ever-faithful wagging tail.

"Your grandma was quite busy with Violet," Molly said. "So I told her I'd take care of Sprinkles for you, and come pick you up once you posted bail."

"Thanks. I really appreciate it, although it would have been nice of my grandma to come. I mean, I understand Violet is having a rough time. But I'm her granddaughter, and I've been accused of murder!"

Molly sighed. "Well, your grandma isn't really taking any of this seriously, because she knows you're innocent. She doesn't see what the big deal is if you have to stay at the station and argue with Mitch for a few hours. You have to understand that almost everyone in Sunshine Springs ends up at the station arguing with Mitch at one point or another. It's almost a hazing ritual that you have to pass to become a Sunshine Springs resident. Think of it as being one step closer to not being an outsider."

I frowned. "That doesn't really make me feel better. What *would* make me feel better is if Mitch would focus on catching the real killer instead of me. And I'm pretty sure that real killer is Todd."

Molly raised an eyebrow. "Todd? The photographer?"

"Yeah. You should have seen him in there. He seemed awfully guilty. He was way too defensive."

"Hmm. Well, I obviously wasn't in there, so I didn't see the way Todd was behaving. But aren't you missing the most obvious suspect in all of this?"

I rubbed my forehead, confused. "Josie? You think Caitlin's own sister would kill her? I know that sort of thing happens, and they did have a big fight. But it didn't seem like that big of a fight. At least not when they were in my pie shop."

"No, not Josie," Molly interrupted. "Theo."

For a few heartbeats, I just stared at Molly. Why hadn't I thought of that myself? It was so obvious, now that she said it. Some great detective I was. Of course Theo was a likely suspect. He had a ton of money—money that all came from his winery as far as I knew—and Caitlin was threatening his winery's reputation, therefore threatening his money. I slapped my forehead with my palm.

"He has the motive for sure. And Caitlin was at the winery earlier in the day, according to what Scott said. Theo must have slipped something into a wine she tasted."

"Bingo."

I frowned. "But I thought you said that you couldn't believe that Theo would take money from the city. If he's so upstanding that he wouldn't even take money from the city, how can you believe that he would commit murder?"

Molly shrugged sheepishly. "Like you said, people can surprise you. I never would have believed it about him, but you have to admit that the circumstances seem awfully damning. It's the only explanation that really makes sense."

"Well, I obviously don't know him well. But you're right: it seems to make the most sense. So what do we do about it? We should tell Mitch, right?"

Molly laughed. "Get in the car."

Feeling somewhat confused, I did as she said.

"But what about Mitch?" I asked as I buckled my seatbelt and Sprinkles hopped into the small backseat. He didn't seem to mind how squashed it was. His tail wagged furiously, and he happily stuck his head in between the driver's seat and passenger's seat, looking back and forth between Molly and me. He gave me a giant, sloppy wet kiss on the cheek, and I had to laugh despite the difficult circumstances I was in.

"Listen," Molly said. "There's a reason that Mitch hasn't contacted Theo, and it's not that he hasn't considered the fact that Theo might be guilty."

Understanding slowly dawned on me, and it only made the sick feeling in my stomach worse. "You mean…"

"Yes. I mean that Mitch is *not* going to confront Theo. Theo is a wealthy, powerful man. And Mitch, well, he's one of those all bark and no bite kind of people. He talks a big talk, and likes to act like he's some sort of tough Wild West Sheriff. But when it comes down to it, he's sort of a fraidy-cat. He knows that crossing Theo would mean having to stand up to Theo. He knows it means facing down Theo's lawyers, who I promise you are the best that money can buy. And he knows that accusing Theo would make him unpopular in town. Most of all, if it's true that Theo is doing some shady money dealings, then it wouldn't surprise me if Mitch was getting some sort of kickback too. In that case, Mitch definitely isn't going to accuse Theo."

None of this boded well for me. "If Theo is so powerful, and has so many people in the town in his back pocket, how are we ever going to prove what he did?"

I was hoping that Molly had some sort of grand plan. She seemed like the sort of person who easily came up with grand plans.

Unfortunately, she didn't have much of a plan at all. She was shaking her head at me, and shrugging her shoulders in that carefree way she had.

"I don't really know the best way to go about this," she said. "But my grandpa always used to say that if you don't know which way to move, sometimes the best thing to do is to just get moving. Maybe you'll go the right way, but if you don't, at least you've eliminated one of the wrong ways."

I stared at her. "What exactly do you mean by that?"

"I mean that we should just get moving. We should just go down to the Sunshine Springs Winery, confront Theo, and see what he says. I figure if he's guilty, it'll probably be pretty obvious by his reaction."

I stared at her some more. "Are you serious? I'm accused of murder, and your best suggestion is to randomly show up at the prime suspect's winery to see if he happens to look guilty?"

Molly chewed her lower lip. "Yeah, that sounded better in my head than it did saying it out loud. But anyway, if you don't have a better suggestion, then I stand by mine. We need to just get moving. Haven't you ever seen any of those crime shows? Evidence disappears quickly. If you want to catch the killer, you have to take action right away."

I hated to admit it, but I supposed she was right. I didn't have a better suggestion, and I was afraid of evidence disappearing. Besides, I was so angry at Theo for potentially ruining my life that I wanted to go confront him and let out some of my anger, even if that confrontation turned out to be pointless.

"Okay. But, right now? It's past nine o'clock at night."

"Exactly. It's perfect timing. We'll catch Theo off guard. He's probably sitting at home in his big fancy villa thinking he got away with murder. He'll be so surprised to see us show up that he might not be able to hide his guilt."

The more we talked about this, the more I had a feeling it wasn't going to go anywhere. But then again, if what Molly was saying about Mitch was true, then sending the police in there was unlikely to be helpful either.

"Okay. Whatever. No time like the present, I guess."

"Atta girl," Molly said as she revved up the engine and peeled out of the police station's parking lot. "Let's go catch us a murderer."

I still couldn't shake the uneasy feeling in my stomach. Were we going to catch a murderer? Or were we going to stir up a hornet's nest and make a murderer very, very angry at us?

I couldn't shake the uneasy feeling that the latter option was more likely.

Chapter Seven

I've always thought that wineries were magical places. Call me one of those big city crazy folks if you want, but it's true. When you're usually surrounded by sky-high buildings, dirty sidewalks, and endless honking horns, the peacefulness of green vines loaded down with juicy grapes, shimmering under the brilliant, hot sun...well, what can I say except that it's magical?

Sunshine Springs Winery seemed more magical than any other winery I'd ever been to. The way the place took my breath away caught me quite by surprise. For one thing, I was coming here for a reason that was anything but magical. That alone should have been enough to temper my enthusiasm for wineries. For another thing, the sun had long since set, leaving the grapevines in darkness. I'd always thought that the sunshine was what really made these places look magical.

I was wrong.

The starlight and moonlight upped the magical factor by about a thousand. As we pulled into the dusty, gravel driveway that led to the winery and its grand tasting room, I couldn't keep myself from gazing in awe.

"Wow," I whispered. I hadn't thought I was speaking loud enough for Molly to hear me, but apparently I was.

"Yeah. 'Wow' is right. Now, try to imagine being a teenage girl, seeing this place, seeing the handsomest boy you've ever met, and knowing that he's the future owner. No wonder we all had huge crushes on him." Molly sighed forlornly, and I couldn't help but laugh.

"Oh, come on. It can't be all that bad that you missed out on him, can it? After all, if you'd married him, you'd now be married to a murderer."

"*Alleged* murderer," Molly corrected. "But anyway, I'm over it. Once I grew up, I realized that there are many more fish in the sea. One day I'll catch one of them, and he'll be so handsome and so wealthy that he'll put Theo to shame. Just you wait, dahhhhling." She dragged out the word darling and fluttered her hand like a lovesick damsel who was about to faint from excitement over her prince.

I rolled my eyes. "Okay, come on, princess. Enough with the theatrics. Let's go get this over with and hope for the best."

I hopped out of the car and Sprinkles followed me. For a moment, I thought about telling him to wait in the car, but then thought better of it. If I was going to confront a murderer, it wouldn't hurt to have a guard dog by my side. Even if that guard dog was named Sprinkles and was about as lovable as they came. I knew that if it came down to it, Sprinkles would protect me. He was friendly to everyone until they crossed me.

My ex-husband had learned that lesson quickly. Laughably, he tried to get custody of Sprinkles in the divorce. I nipped that one in the bud by letting him keep Sprinkles by himself one night. Sprinkles had spent the whole night growling and barking at him, taking breaks only to pee on his furniture and tear up a few of his favorite expensive dress shirts. Yeah, I won that round in the divorce negotiations for sure.

Molly and I were silent as we crept toward the tasting room. We weren't planning to break in. We were just going to take a quick look around the outside and see if anything looked suspicious. Then we'd continue on down the path that led up to the private residence behind the tasting room. We'd knock on the door, confront Theo, and hope for the best. Still, I felt like some sort of criminal as I crept down the path and peered into the tasting room's large front windows. I imagined that if Theo saw us now, he wouldn't be too happy with what we were doing.

But I soon forgot about my worries. Once I peered in the window, I couldn't think about anything else except how beautiful the tasting room was. The inside appeared elegantly rustic. It looked like some sort of magical forest with rough-hewn wooden furniture, lush greenery everywhere, and expensive chandeliers. Sounds weird, I know. But somehow, it worked.

"Wow," I said for what must have been the tenth time since we drove onto the property. "I know you said you're over him, but I can't help thinking that whatever girl he did marry was just a teeny bit lucky. Especially since, if he goes to jail, she'll probably get to take control of all of this. Not a bad deal if you ask me."

Molly snorted. "I'm not sure that's exactly how things work when the owner of a winery goes to jail. I don't know. You're the lawyer, so you tell me. But anyway, it's a moot point. Theo never married. There is no lucky girl. Or no unlucky one, for that matter."

"Ha. So Mr. Tough Guy managed to avoid settling down. Maybe he should have found a girl. She might have kept him a little bit more on the straight and narrow, and he might never have murdered someone."

In the moonlight, I saw Molly roll her eyes. "All right, enough playing. Let's confront this guy."

We marched up the gravel pathway with Sprinkles guarding our rear. But we lost the element of surprise much sooner than I'd hoped. As soon as we had taken about ten steps down the path, we hit some sort of motion sensors. All around us, lights came on and illuminated the pathway. From somewhere inside the house, a dog barked. I turned back to look at Sprinkles, and saw his ears perking up.

"No, Sprinkles," I pleaded desperately. "Whatever you do, please don't bark right now."

For once, Sprinkles listened. He gave an annoyed grunt, but otherwise kept quiet and continued to follow Molly and me as we made our way toward the now brilliantly lighted front door.

We'd only made it about halfway down the long path before that front door flew open. A large, muscular silhouette stood in the open doorway, and I had never felt as naked while fully clothed as I did right then. I felt completely awkward and exposed. This was a ridiculous idea. What were we doing? I shouldn't have let Molly talk me into coming here without calling the police first. I was wanted for murder, for goodness' sake.

Of course, I was innocent. But it wasn't going to look good that I was sneaking around in the middle of the night. My mind started racing, and I started to contemplate turning around and running. I could probably get out of here before Theo realized who I was. I was new in town, after all. It was dark, and he wouldn't know who I was. Sprinkles would be a problem. Dalmatians weren't all that common, and if Theo asked around town he would probably learn who owned a Dalmatian. But still, I might get away with it, if he didn't pay much attention to the dog.

"Molly?" the silhouette shouted. "Molly Taylor, is that you?"

I groaned. So much for making a quick getaway. Theo knew Molly, and I wasn't going to leave Molly here alone. Even though this had been her crazy idea, she was only doing it to try to help me. I had to stick it out with her. I owed her at least that much.

"Yes, it's me," Molly shouted. "Call off your dogs, or we'll be forced to sic ours on you."

I looked at Molly in consternation. "Molly!" I hissed. "Don't say that. I don't want Sprinkles to have to fight. I'm not sure what kind of dog Theo has. What if it's a pit bull? I don't think Sprinkles can take on a pit bull."

Molly gave me an exasperated look. "Don't tell me that you're one of those people who misjudge pit bulls. You know that they're perfectly lovable. They just need good training."

"Okay, okay. You're right. I shouldn't pick on pit bulls specifically. But whatever kind of dog Theo has, he's probably trained it to kill first and ask questions later. He seems like that kind of man."

"You're overreacting. Come on. He's not that kind of man at all. Let's just go talk to him."

"He's not that kind of man? Molly, we think he murdered someone! What kind of man do you think he is?"

But Molly didn't answer me. She was already marching down the path toward Theo's front door. I sighed and followed her, thankful that Sprinkles was right on my heels even though I hoped he didn't have to fight.

When we got up to the door, any worries I'd had about whether this was a mistake were confirmed. This was *definitely* a mistake.

Theo was the most muscular man I'd ever seen. He was even more muscular than Sheriff Mitch. What did the guys in this town do? Spend every spare moment at the gym, seeing who could bench press more? Well, if that was the case, then Theo would beat out Mitch. And that was saying something, because Mitch looked like he could hold his own pretty well in a weightlifting competition.

But it wasn't the muscles that scared me the most. It was the irritated, angry look on his face. Molly hadn't been kidding when she said he was good-looking. Yes, he was a few years older than me, but he wore his age well. I could see how he would have been a total heartthrob in high school. His dark Italian features were enough to make any girl swoon.

He smiled at Molly, but his smile didn't reach his eyes. And it was those eyes that really scared me. They were dark, and looked angrier than I'd ever seen eyes look before. But now was not the time to panic. I was here, and it was too late to change that. At least I had my guard Dalmatian behind me. Even if his name was Sprinkles, I knew he would fight fiercely for me. I also had my hand on my phone in my pocket. I could call 911 at a moment's notice. Mitch might be a jerk, but surely the police here weren't big enough jerks that they would let Theo kill someone in cold blood. If I made an emergency call, they'd send someone out to save us. Wouldn't they?

"Theo Russo," Molly said as she put her hands on her hips. Apparently this arrogant side of him was enough to give her a fresh burst of angry courage.

He smirked at her. "Yes? It's been a while since you've shown up on my doorstep in the middle of the night. A couple decades, I think. I thought you'd given up that desperate act. To what do I owe this pleasure?"

"This isn't a social call, Theo," Molly said. "I'm here because I know what you did to that journalist. You can either go confess it all to Mitch right now, or my lawyer friend here is going to present all the evidence against you in court. And trust me, you don't want that. You know how these things go. If you confess beforehand, you can make a deal with the judge and get a lighter sentence. But if you make things difficult, you'll end up with life in prison. Possibly even the death penalty. California still has that, you know?"

Theo was either innocent, or the best actor I'd ever seen. He looked genuinely confused and shocked by Molly's words. "What on earth are you talking about?"

Molly faltered slightly. I supposed his act was working pretty well on her, and I decided it was time for me to jump in. I hadn't wanted her to present me as a lawyer, since I wasn't a criminal lawyer. Not only that, but I was a suspect in the case. I was pretty sure there were rules that disallowed a murder suspect from bringing a case against another suspect in the same murder. But now wasn't the time to worry about technicalities like that.

I drew myself up to my full height, which still wasn't much against Theo's height. But I did the best I could to look imposing.

"What Molly is talking about is the fact that you poisoned Caitlin Dixon because she found out that you were stealing money from the city and blackmailing City Council members."

Theo looked at me with some mixture of curiosity, amusement, and disdain. I think disdain was probably winning out in that mix.

"This has to do with Caitlin Dixon?" His voice took on a decidedly more antagonistic tone than it had had a moment ago. "She sent you here?" He looked at Molly. "Really, Molly. I don't know what this is about, but I would have thought better of you. You don't seem like the type to work with an annoying, squawking parrot like that Caitlin girl."

"Oh, don't try to play dumb," Molly said, seeming to regain her composure. "That 'annoying squawking parrot,' as you call her, is dead thanks to you. We all know it was you. You wanted to get rid of her so that she wouldn't discover the truth about your winery."

Theo's eyes widened. "Wait a minute? Caitlin's actually dead? Really? I've been hiding out in my villa all day, trying to avoid her until she heads back to San Francisco."

Molly looked uncertain again. "Yes, she's dead. She was poisoned yesterday, as you well know."

Theo let out a whoop of excitement. This was so unexpected that I nearly jumped out of my skin. Molly and Sprinkles looked just as startled.

"That's the best news I've heard all day," Theo said. Molly and I just stared at him. Who in their right mind gave a whoop of excitement when they heard that someone had died? Theo seemed in that moment to realize his mistake.

"I mean, of course that's horrible. I'm sorry to hear that that young lady has passed away. But I have to admit it does make my life easier. She was over here sticking her nose in everything, trying to find a scandal that doesn't exist!" He slammed his fist against the doorframe angrily, and I jumped again.

"I don't see why you're so happy," Molly said, trying again to make him understand why we were there. "You're the prime suspect. You're the one who had the most motivation to get rid of her."

Theo raised an eyebrow at Molly. "If I'm the prime suspect, then why haven't the police come here to arrest me?"

He had a point, and Molly knew it. But she wasn't giving up that easily. "You know why they haven't arrested you, Theo. You have Mitch and that whole Police Department in your back pocket. You think money can get you out of any problem. But let me tell you, money isn't going to let you get away with murder! My friend and I are going to prove you did it. And when we do, you're going to wish you had just 'fessed up in the first place."

Theo looked at me as though seeing me for the first time. "Are you really a lawyer?"

He looked doubtfully at my clothing. I wasn't wearing my Drunken Pie apron anymore, but I still had on the flour-covered pants and shirt I'd worn to work all day today. I didn't exactly look like some sort of high-powered lawyer. I looked more like the pie shop owner that I was. But I wasn't going to let Molly down, and I wasn't going to let Theo intimidate me. Technically, I was a lawyer. I might not be working for a law firm anymore, and I might not be a criminal lawyer, but I *was* a lawyer. That much was true.

"Yes, I'm a lawyer. And I advise you to cooperate and go confess to the police, or it's going to be much worse for you."

Theo scowled at me. "Well, if you are a lawyer, then you can talk to my lawyer once I'm arrested and charged with this murder. Otherwise, I would appreciate it if you ladies got off my property. This is a private residence, and the tasting room is closed right now. Feel free to come back tomorrow during our business hours and try some wine."

With that, he slammed the door in our faces. Somewhere back in his house, his dogs had started barking again. Sprinkles growled, and this time I didn't bother telling him to be quiet. Who cared if he barked? Theo knew we were here, and if he was going to sic his dogs on us, he would have done it by now.

"Come on," I said to Molly. "This was pointless. I don't think we learned anything, and all we did was piss off Theo."

"It wasn't pointless," Molly insisted, even though she looked just as dejected as I did. "Did you see how he acted? He was a bit too ridiculous. He was trying to act surprised, and then happy when he learned that Caitlin was dead. He probably figured that no real murderer would act happy. They'd be too afraid that acting happy would make them look guilty, right? So he was using some reverse psychology crap on us to convince us he's innocent when really he's not."

To be honest, I wasn't sure whether Theo was smart enough to use reverse psychology crap on us. He struck me as a big, unintelligent oaf. Sure, he was good-looking and muscular, but just because he was wealthy and owned a successful winery, that didn't mean he was smart. I didn't think that someone who was actually smart would admit to being happy that someone had died, especially not when there was good reason for people to suspect him of murder. Perhaps Theo wasn't so much using reverse psychology crap as much as he was just overconfident and thought that no one could actually pin the murder on him.

Or perhaps, I myself had had my thinking clouded by my determination to figure out whom besides myself to pin the murder on. In any case, I felt that there was certainly more here to explore. I decided I would come back after my pie shop closed the next day and pay a visit to the Sunshine Springs Winery's tasting room. Theo had given me an invitation, after all. I would take him up on that invitation, and with any luck, I would make him regret the day that he gave me that invitation.

I'd been screwed over too many times by men in my life, and enough was enough. There was no way that I was going to let Theo Russo get away with murder and blame me for it. He was about to find out that there was a whole lot more to this pie shop owner than just butter, sugar, and flour.

Chapter Eight

The Sunshine Springs Winery looked different in the daylight, but no less magical. The grapevines shimmered in the sunlight in that way I loved, and as I drove up the gravel road and parked my small, worn down coupe in the dusty parking lot, I almost forgot that I was there to try to catch a murderer. Sprinkles sat in the passenger seat next to me, and he seemed decidedly less enthralled by the view of the grapevines. He let out a low growl as I parked, as though still remembering the drama of the night before.

"I know, boy," I said. "This place didn't get off to a very good start for you and me. But I have to see if I can find out what's really going on with this Theo character."

With a resigned sigh, I opened my car door and started to climb out. Sprinkles followed me, sticking close to my heels as I walked toward the tasting room's entrance. When we got there, I turned and shook my head at him.

"Sorry, boy. You'll have to stay out there. They don't allow dogs in the tasting room."

Sprinkles whined, clearly unhappy with the situation, but he didn't protest too much. He sat down by the door like a sentry, his sharp eyes darting back and forth across the grapevines, as though he expected mortal danger to appear at any moment.

I had to admit that I felt better knowing he was out here. He was a good dog, and as long as nothing crazy happened, he would sit still and not bother anyone. But if anyone inside tried to hurt me, he would hear and come rushing in to help. I wasn't sure whether I was being paranoid by assuming that I might be attacked at a fancy tasting room during business hours, but given the events of the last day or two, I'd rather be overly paranoid than not paranoid enough.

I marched into the tasting room, my head held high as I prepared to confront Theo yet again. But Theo wasn't in the tasting room. I shouldn't have been surprised by this. What had I been thinking? That the owner of the winery spent his days mindlessly pouring out samples for slightly tipsy tourists? No, he'd hired people to do that for him, of course. Those people were standing behind the gleaming wooden counter right now, flashing overly enthusiastic smiles at their last customers of the day.

I didn't know everyone in town well enough to recognize them by sight yet, but I knew enough to know that no one currently in the room was a local. Their overly trendy clothes and syrupy sweet laughs gave them away as tourists from the "big city" who had come to spend a sunny day in wine country.

All except one person. To my surprise, there was one local, and that local was Violet Murphy. I hadn't seen Violet since she left the police station with Grams the night that Mitch accused Josie, Todd and me of murder, but Grams had texted me to tell me that the poor woman was on her last frayed nerve. I'd been annoyed with Grams for worrying more about Violet than about me, but I supposed I shouldn't have been too surprised. Grams was always there for me when I really needed her, but she had never coddled me. And since she didn't think Mitch's accusations were all that serious, allowing me to whine about the bad week I was having would amount to nothing more than coddling in her eyes.

Nothing made Grams angrier than when she thought I was playing the victim. I'd had plenty of opportunities in my life to play the victim, not the least of which was when my parents both died in a car wreck while I was still finishing up college. Grams herself could have spent a long time feeling sorry for herself over that tragedy. After all, my father had been her son, so the loss was just as great for her as it was for me. But she had been my strength during that time, choosing to focus on happy memories and the time she did have with her son instead of losing herself in grief. She had been my rock, and the only thing that got me through.

Now, I should take heart at the fact that she didn't think my current situation was a tragedy. But I couldn't help thinking that her blasé attitude had more to do with the fact that she didn't truly understand the seriousness of a murder charge than with her truly knowing that it was no big deal. In any case, whether she was right or wrong, she had chosen to focus on taking care of Violet instead of taking care of me.

Grams had told me that Violet had been horribly shaky, and hadn't wanted to drive anymore. Honestly, I wasn't sure whether Violet should be driving. Sure, she hadn't actually been responsible for Caitlin's death. But she still should have been able to stop before running over Caitlin's head when Caitlin fell into the street. The speed limit on Main Street was twenty-five miles per hour, and from what I'd seen, most of the residents were surprisingly good at obeying the speed limit. Violet couldn't have been going that fast when Caitlin fell into the street, so Violet must not have been paying very good attention to what was going on around her as she drove.

But I supposed I should go easy on the old woman. Whether she should be driving or not, Violet had been through an ordeal. There was no denying that. And she'd already been such a nervous wreck from what I'd seen that it was a wonder the whole situation hadn't pushed her completely over the edge.

As I watched Violet now, she looked calmer than I'd ever seen her. Her hand still shook as she raised her wine glass and took a sip, but her face—at least as much of it as I could see from her side profile—looked serene. I decided to go sit by her. I hadn't spoken to her since Caitlin's death, and she might have seen something in the pie shop that would be helpful. I didn't really think that Josie or Todd were the ones who had killed Caitlin. At this point, my money was on Theo. He had the strongest motive, and he'd acted a little too crazy for my liking the night before. Something about him just didn't sit right with me. But if I was going to play detective, I should explore all leads. Since I was here at the same time as Violet, I might as well see if she could tell me anything helpful. I just had to be careful not to upset her too much. If Grams got wind of the fact that I was stirring up Violet, I'd be sure to get an earful.

I slipped into the barstool next to Violet and flashed her a wide smile. "Hi, Violet. Funny running into you here. But I'm glad to see you out. How are you feeling today? Grams told me that it's been a rough time for you."

Violet seemed startled by my presence. She looked at me with what almost could have been called a scowl, but she managed to smooth away the scowl pretty quickly. I couldn't blame her for not wanting to see me. After all, I was just one more reminder of the chaos that had filled her life in the last two days.

"I'm fine, dear," she said as she lifted her wine glass and took a healthy swig from it. "Just having a glass of my favorite Pinot to try to relax. This whole ordeal has been so upsetting."

"I'm sure it has," I said sympathetically. "I hope you know that I had nothing to do with Caitlin's death. In fact, I'm doing my best to help the police figure out who really did kill her."

Violet didn't look comforted by this news. She frowned at me, and took another long swig from her wine glass before replying. "I'm willing to give you the benefit of the doubt that you didn't kill that girl. You are Agnes' granddaughter, after all, even if you're an outsider. But really, dear. Don't you think it's best to leave the murder investigation to the police? Chasing after a murderer sounds dangerous. I certainly wouldn't want my granddaughter involved in something like that."

I frowned. I should have expected an answer like that. Grams herself had hinted at the fact that I was better off letting Mitch handle this. But I didn't trust Mitch, and I wasn't leaving my fate in the hands of a corrupt, small-town sheriff who saw me as nothing more than an outsider who deserved to be burned at the stake. I highly doubted, however, that I was going to convince Violet that the investigation was better off in my hands than the Sheriff's. I ignored the comment, and decided instead to ask her about whether she'd seen anything at the Drunken Pie Café.

"Oh, don't worry. I'll be careful not to get myself involved in anything too dangerous. But since I saw you here, I was just wondering if you'd happened to have seen anything suspicious when you were at the pie shop before Caitlin died."

Violet started shaking a bit more violently. "I didn't see anything, dear. I wasn't paying attention to what was going on at Caitlin's table. I don't generally make a habit of eavesdropping on my neighbors whenever I'm out at a restaurant."

I sighed. I guess I hadn't expected much from her, but it would have been nice if she'd suddenly remembered that she'd seen Todd or Josie slip something into Caitlin's drink. Of course, if she did remember something that obvious, she would have already told Mitch. I'd been intending to press her a little bit and see if I could jog her memory more than the police might have already, but when I saw how badly she was shaking, I thought better of it.

"Don't worry about it," I told her. "Just enjoy your wine and relax. In fact, I could use a glass of wine myself. This whole thing has been stressful for me, too. I'm assuming they serve by the glass here, since you're having a glass. What do you recommend?"

"No, actually. They don't generally serve by the glass. They only do that for locals who know enough to ask for it. Most of the tourists come in here and do a tasting, and then that's it." Violet frowned at me. "You're not exactly a local. But you are Agnes' granddaughter. I suppose I could vouch for you enough to get you a glass of wine, if that's what you want. I'd recommend the 2016 reserve pinot. It was their best year, in my opinion. You might think I'm just a crazy old lady, and perhaps you're right. But trust me, dear. I've drunk enough wine in my life to know when a pinot is excellent. The Sunshine Springs' 2016 reserve is excellent."

Violet waved over one of the tasting room's employees and told him to get me a glass.

He gave Violet a strange look, and I supposed he wasn't happy about having to serve me a glass instead of the standard tasting menu.

"A glass of the special 2016 reserve?" he asked. "Really?"

Violet gave him a sharp look. "I'm not asking for any super special treatment. Just a glass of the same 2016 reserve that I drink. You've already got a bottle open for me, so it shouldn't be too much trouble. And this girl is a friend of mine."

The employee looked chastised. "Right, sorry. Just wanted to make sure I understood. I'll get her a glass of what you're drinking right away."

A minute or so later, I had a giant glass of wine sitting in front of me. The employee must have poured a quarter of the bottle into my cup. Maybe he was trying to make up for his initial hesitation over Violet's request that he serve me by the glass.

"Cheers," Violet said as she raised her drink.

"Cheers," I replied, and clinked my glass with hers. I felt somewhat heartened by the small gesture she'd made of ordering a glass of wine for me. Each new little gesture like that brought me one step closer to being a local instead of an outsider in Sunshine Springs. And right now, I could really use local status.

Heartened by Violet's small act of trust, I decided to see whether she would be willing to talk to me about Theo. I had to be careful. Many of the locals loved Theo, and if she was one of them, I didn't want to get on her bad side by slandering him. But anything that I could learn about him would make this trip out to the tasting room a little less pointless. I took a deep breath, and decided to try my luck.

"So," I began. "You come out here a lot, huh?"

Violet raised an eyebrow at me. "Are you trying to accuse me of being a lush?"

I blushed. "Oh, certainly not," I stammered. "I only meant that it seems like a nice place, and you seem very knowledgeable about the wine. As a newcomer to Sunshine Springs, I'd be interested in learning a little more about the history of this place."

This explanation seemed to satisfy Violet. She smiled and got a wistful look in her eyes. "This place has quite a history, let me tell you. Theo's father started this winery back when I was a young woman. He was a pull yourself up by the bootstraps kind of guy, and he quickly made a big success of the vineyard. All the locals were so proud of him, myself included. In fact, if you look on the wall over there, that picture on the top right is of him and me during one of the many wine festivals he threw for the locals in Sunshine Springs. He used to have parties all the time to show the locals he appreciated them."

I looked at the wall where she was pointing. Several photographs and mementos from the winery's history had been arranged into an attractive collage all up and down the wall. The picture Violet was pointing to showed her as a younger woman, and I easily recognized Theo's father. The resemblance was uncanny. In the photograph, the elder Russo couldn't have been much older than Theo was now. He grinned at the camera, and one arm slung lazily around Violet's young shoulders. His other arm was raised so he could give the camera a thumbs up.

"He looks like he was a really nice guy," I said.

Violet sighed. "He was a character, that's for sure. But a smart, wealthy character. He knew how to run a vineyard better than anyone in wine country. Theo has done well with the winery too, of course. But his father was the one who gave this place its wings. It really is the pride and joy of Sunshine Springs. It holds its own against the other big-name wineries in wine country, and it put our little town on the map."

"It's a great place. Why don't you think Theo has been quite as good at running the winery as his father?" I prodded.

I watched Violet carefully, wondering if my statement would hit any nerves. Did she know anything about any shady deals Theo might be involved in? She'd been around the town for a while, and from the way she was talking, she liked to spend a lot of time at the winery. Perhaps she had seen something to give her pause, and that was why she thought Theo wasn't as good of a businessman as his father.

Violet's eyes darkened. She must have seen through my attempt to sound innocent in my questioning. "Don't tell me you buy into what that Caitlin girl was selling. I said Theo wasn't as good as his dad at the business, yes. All that means is that his father was extremely exceptional. Theo is also good. It's just hard for anyone to live up to how amazing his father was. I certainly didn't mean that Theo is doing anything shady like those maggots from the big city think."

I was surprised by the vehemence in Violet's voice, although I shouldn't have been. The Sunshine Springs locals were extremely protective of their own. Theo was one of their own, even if I did think he was a murderer. But since I'd already upset Violet, and she'd seen through my ruse anyway, I decided I might as well press her on the point a little bit.

"But don't you think it's at least a little bit suspicious that the girl who was investigating a possible scandal here suddenly ends up poisoned? If you assume that there was truth to the rumors Caitlin was investigating, then it explains why someone would have had motive to murder her. It's the only motive that makes sense, if you ask me. People don't generally go around killing other people for no reason, and protecting a family winery's fortune seems like a much stronger reason to commit murder than, say, an argument between sisters over whom one of those sisters was dating."

Violet's eyes turned into storm clouds as she looked at me. Her hands stopped shaking, and her voice was surprisingly steady and strong as she spoke. "You watch yourself, Izzy. You have no idea what you're talking about. Theo is a good man, and there's no scandal here to find. That's why he isn't a murder suspect. Mitch knows everyone on the City Council well, and he can request the Council's financial records as evidence at any time. He knows that Theo isn't hiding anything, and if Theo had nothing to hide, then he had no reason to murder Caitlin."

"I'm sorry," I backtracked. "I didn't mean to upset you. I'm just trying to find an explanation for all of this that makes sense. And the Josie theory doesn't make sense. Neither does the Todd theory.

What motivation did they really have? Theo was under attack by Caitlin. That makes it seem as though he had motivation. And from what I understand, Caitlin spent a good deal of time here at the winery the day she died. It would have been the perfect opportunity for someone to slip something poisonous into her drink. It just seems strange to me that Theo isn't under investigation at all. It seems like a cover-up."

I knew that what I was saying was only going to make Violet angrier, but I had to say it. I had to see what her reaction was. If she sat here all the time as she'd said, she might know something. Perhaps she was hiding it out of loyalty to Theo, because he was a local. Perhaps she would say something that would give away what she knew.

Instead, she slammed her fist on the table with surprising force, causing me to jump. She pointed a finger at me, her hand shaking violently again as it always did, but her voice remaining steady.

"Theo is not a suspect because there's no evidence against him. He has nothing to hide. I'll tell you who has something to hide. It's that girl's sister, Josie. I was in here for part of the time that Josie, Todd and Caitlin were all in here. The three of them were arguing almost constantly. Oh, they tried to act friendly when they thought they were being watched. And I suppose there were some moments of genuine camaraderie between them. But the arguing far outweighed the friendliness. Caitlin spent all of her time either asking ridiculous questions about Theo, or yelling at her sister for being there and for dating Todd. At one point, when Caitlin was busy questioning one of the tasting room employees about Theo, I saw that Josie girl pull a bottle of pills out of her purse. She took a big pill, ground it up, and dropped the ground up powder into Caitlin's wine glass. I didn't say anything, because I never assumed it was poison. I figured, given how crazy Caitlin was acting, that perhaps Josie was trying to give her some sort of anti-anxiety medicine or something to relax her. But later, when Caitlin ended up dead from poison, I realized that whatever Josie gave her must not have been so benign."

My jaw hung open "Are you serious? You actually saw Josie putting something into Caitlin's glass? Why didn't you tell someone?"

"Well, now I've told someone. Now, I've told the police, like any normal person does when they have evidence regarding a murder investigation. I'm not interested in trying to play detective like you are. I only wish that I'd said something sooner. Then maybe that poor girl might still be alive. Now, if you'll excuse me, I'm done discussing this. I hope you'll at least take comfort in the fact that what I've told Mitch about Josie should help clear your name. But I don't want to talk about it anymore. It's so upsetting. And I don't want to hear any more of this nonsense about Theo being a murderer. He's a good man, and a pillar in this community. If you know what's good for you, you'll stop making ridiculous accusations against him."

Violet quickly chugged the last sip of her wine, then slammed the glass down and slid off her barstool in a shaky, awkward movement. I reflexively reached out to grab her and help, but she batted me away angrily.

"Don't touch me. I don't want any part with anyone who would falsely accuse someone of murder. Josie is the real criminal here, and Mitch will see to it that she comes to justice. You should stick to baking pies and leave the detective work to the real detectives."

With that, Violet shakily stormed out of the tasting room. I stared after her for a few moments, trying to process everything that she'd just told me. If what she'd said was true, Josie might very well be responsible for Caitlin's death. But was it really possible? Out of all the possible suspects—Theo, Josie and Todd—Josie seemed like the least likely to have committed the murder.

I didn't know what the relationship between Josie and Caitlin was really like, but for someone to be angry enough to kill their own sister, I assumed they would need to be angry enough not to be hanging out with her on a work assignment. Unless Josie had been pretending to get along with Caitlin somewhat in order to get close enough to her sister to do the deed.

With a sigh, I gulped down the rest of my wine. It almost seemed a crime to gulp down such a delicious wine. I had to admit that the Sunshine Springs 2016 reserve pinot was one of the best I'd ever tasted. Still, just because Theo could make a good pinot didn't mean he wasn't a murderer.

No matter what Violet had seen Josie do, and no matter how vigorously Violet defended Theo, I wasn't quite ready to let go of him as a suspect yet. The tasting room was closing for the day, so I stood and headed toward the door. But I would be back. I would figure out a way to get more information about Theo, and I would figure out how all of these confusing threads tied together.

I just had to do it before the murderer figured out a way to completely cover his or her tracks. And I had to do it before Mitch found a way to pin the murder on me. No small task perhaps, but I was quickly learning that nothing was quite as motivating as the prospect of spending life in prison for a crime you didn't commit.

Chapter Nine

The next two days were relatively uneventful, although the pie shop was surprisingly busy. It seemed that Molly had been right: once people tasted the pie, they weren't able to stay away. Not even the fact that I was a suspect in a murder case could keep people from stopping by to try a peach brandy cobbler or a strawberry moonshine pie. Business was booming, and as long as I could clear my name in the end, it looked like being accused of murder might have been the best thing that could've happened for my little business.

I hadn't had a chance to go back to the Sunshine Springs Winery, and I hadn't had a chance to discuss things with Molly, either. The library was having a book fair this week, so Molly was just as busy as I was. We were planning to catch up on the weekend, but in the meantime, I was left on my own to ponder the meager clues I had.

As another day at the Drunken Pie Café came to an end, and the crowd of customers dwindled down, I was happy to look up and see a familiar, friendly face walking through the front door. The bells above the door jingled to announce that Scott was walking in with a delivery. I hadn't seen him since Mitch had kicked him out of the police station, and seeing his warm smile now boosted my spirits more than I would have thought possible. My heart warmed as he grinned at me, and I felt a little bit of an electric rush zoom through my body.

I forced myself to push away thoughts of how handsome he was. Now was not the time to be ruining one of my only friendships in town with a silly crush. Besides, I wasn't exactly ready for another relationship. My divorce had yet to be finalized. That would happen tomorrow, actually, and I figured I should settle into my new life as a single woman and business owner before I started thinking about men again. Not to mention, I should probably focus on clearing my name of murder before I focused on getting a date.

I could still look though, right? And boy, was Scott a looker.

"Afternoon," he called out, completely oblivious to the embarrassing thoughts that were running through my head at the moment. "I have a delivery for you. Must be to-go cups. The box is super light."

"Oh, good. I'm almost out of to-go cups. It's amazing how quickly my little business has taken off. Being accused of murder apparently does wonders for your bottom line."

Scott laughed, but then his face turned serious. "Speaking of that...I have some news you might be interested in."

I leaned across the counter, hoping that he was about to tell me that some evidence had turned up to prove that Theo was the murderer. Or perhaps Josie had been proven to be the killer. I knew Violet had talked to Mitch about the pills Josie had supposedly put in Caitlin's drink, but nothing had come of that as far as I'd heard. Maybe Violet was just a crazy old lady, and Mitch had known better than to put much stock in what she said. But in any case, before Scott could get out another word, the bell above the door was jingling again. I turned to greet my customer somewhat reluctantly. I should be grateful for any business I got, but at the moment I didn't want any more customers. I wanted to know what Scott had to say.

When my eyes fell on the woman entering the pie shop, though, I realized that she wasn't here to buy a slice of pie.

Josie Dixon was storming into my café, looking as though she was ready to kill me. I shivered slightly. It was possible, according to Violet at least, that Josie was the murderer. And if she had killed her own sister, what was to stop her from killing me? I cringed, glad that Scott was in the shop as well. Surely, Josie was not going to murder me in cold blood with an eyewitness standing right there. Grams had taken Sprinkles for the day again, and I wished she hadn't. Maybe I needed to just keep Sprinkles at the shop here with me until this murder case got sorted out.

"You!" Josie screeched at me. Her cheeks had turned almost purple with anger.

"Josie," I said, trying to keep my voice as calm and neutral as possible. "What can I do for you?"

"What can you do for me?" she spat out. "You can go confess to this murder, so I can get back to my life and move on from this whole horrible situation!"

I frowned at her. "Josie, I didn't kill your sister. I'm sorry for your loss. Truly, I am. But I swear to you that I had nothing to do with her death."

"I don't believe you!" Josie yelled. "I have no idea what you had against my sister, but you had to have been the one who poisoned her. I don't know how you did it, but somehow you put something in her food!"

"Josie, I swear I didn't do it," I repeated. "What reason would I have to kill your sister? You should be talking to Theo over at the winery. He's the one your sister was investigating. He's the one who stood to lose a lot. Why isn't anyone going after the only one with the real motivation to kill Caitlin?"

I threw my hands up in exasperation. Apparently, even Josie didn't think Theo was guilty.

"Theo didn't know we were coming to the winery that day," Josie retorted. "We purposely kept our visit secret until we got there. Caitlin wanted to catch him off guard in hopes that he wouldn't be able to hide his guilt if we surprised him with sudden accusations."

I almost laughed. Apparently, Caitlin had been trying the same thing on Theo that I had: attempting to surprise him into admitting guilt.

"And?" I asked, unable to keep the sarcasm out of my voice. "Did it work?"

Josie narrowed her eyes at me. "I don't know. I didn't think that Caitlin was able to get anything truly damning out of Theo that day. He was definitely surprised that we were there, and he was angry at Caitlin's accusations. But to me, he did a pretty good job of acting innocent. In any case, by the time he realized we were there, we had already all had a full round of tastings. It was too late for him to put anything in our drinks. If he wanted to poison us, he would've had to have done it another day when he had more time. Which means it must have been you. For some reason, you poisoned her food when we came to your pie shop!"

"Josie, you're not making any sense. I had no time to prepare a poison either! I didn't know you were coming to my pie shop that day. And even if I had, what motivation did I have to kill your sister?"

"I don't know! That's what I'm here to find out." Josie raised an accusing finger and pointed it in my direction. "You ruined my life, you know that? My sister is dead, the love of my life broke up with me, and I can't even leave Sunshine Springs without getting permission from the sheriff or he's going to think I'm trying to run away from a murder accusation!"

"Todd broke up with you?" I asked, ignoring for the moment the fact that she was screaming at me and accusing me of murder.

She let out an exasperated sigh. "Yes! He told me that he loves me, but that this whole ordeal is too much drama for him. He said he doesn't want to date someone who gets him tangled up in a murder investigation."

I considered this information. I remembered thinking that Todd was acting guilty when we were first accused of murder down at the police station. But over the last few days, he had fallen to the bottom of my suspect list. Theo had a much greater motivation to kill Caitlin, and if what Violet said about Josie was true, then there was some possible evidence that Josie had been the one responsible for the poisoning. The only motivation Todd would have had to kill Caitlin was Caitlin's interference in his relationship with Josie. But surely, if he had killed Caitlin for Josie, then he wouldn't have broken up with Josie after Caitlin's death.

Unless, of course, he was nervous about being caught. Maybe he thought that breaking up with Josie would make him look like a less likely suspect. I chewed my lower lip in frustration as Josie started yelling at me again. I had no strong evidence against anyone, and I was getting more frustrated with every day that passed. I needed to figure out a way to definitively prove that someone else had committed the murder. But there was no hard evidence against anyone, and I felt like the more I learned about Caitlin and the whole situation, the cloudier everything became.

Theo was still my top suspect, but if what Josie said was true, and he hadn't had time to actually poison Caitlin, perhaps it had been Todd after all. Or perhaps Violet was right and it had been Josie. Josie might be trying to cover her own tracks right now. This whole thing was so confusing.

"Are you even listening to me?" Josie yelled. Her angry screeching drew me back to the present moment. But before I could figure out what to say to her, she had run out of patience and was lunging across the counter at me. Her hands reached for my neck, and before I could react she was starting to squeeze tightly, cutting off my airflow. I struggled against her, shocked that someone so petite could be so strong. She was in a rage, and for a moment I panicked. Was I going to be able to get her off of me?

Before I could panic too much, I heard a strong, deep voice yelling at Josie. I had forgotten that Scott was in the room, but I was so glad that he was.

"Hey!" he yelled. "Get off of her!"

The next thing I knew, Scott had grabbed Josie's hands and pried them away from my neck. He gave her a shove across the room, sending her tumbling backward into one of the café tables. She shrieked as chairs went flying, but Scott paid her no mind. He turned to me, concern etched deeply into his eyes.

"Are you all right?" he asked.

Shaken, I nodded. "I...I think so."

I rubbed my neck, which felt tender where Josie's fingers had been. I had a feeling I was going to have bruises there tomorrow, but Josie hadn't done any serious damage. She had, however, brutally attacked me.

Suddenly, I was moving her back up to the top of my suspect list. If she was willing to try to choke me, did that mean she was willing to poison someone? Had she been willing to poison her own sister? I looked over at her with disgust. She was on her hands and knees on the floor of the pie shop, cursing at me and cursing at Scott. Her purse had flown out of her hand, and its contents were everywhere. She was scrambling to pick them up and put them back into her black leather bag.

"Look what you did!" she yelled. "This is all your fault! You've made a complete mess of everything!"

I glanced at Scott, who was scowling at her. I wasn't sure if she was talking to me or Scott—or both—but I wanted her out of my store. Overcome with a sudden burst of anger, I hopped over the counter and kicked her wallet across the floor toward her.

"Get out!" I yelled. "Get your stuff, and get out! I don't want to see you in my pie shop again. I didn't kill your sister, and strangling me isn't going to bring her back!"

Josie looked up at me with an angry scowl, then grabbed her wallet and threw it into her bag. As she reached for a small notebook that had fallen out of her purse, I realized that a small, unmarked bottle that looked like a pill bottle had also fallen out of her purse. It was under a chair that she had her back to at the moment.

My pulse quickened. Was that the same bottle of pills that Violet had seen her using at the winery the day Caitlin died? Was it possible that Violet had been right, and Josie had poisoned her sister?

As quickly as I could, I strode past Josie, bent down to pick up the bottle, and slipped it into my apron pocket. I walked back around the counter and stood there as she threw everything back into her purse.

She was angry, and never stopped cursing at me. She didn't seem to miss the bottle of pills, and once she had looked around and made sure that nothing else from her purse remained on the floor, she stood and kicked one of the chairs that had fallen, causing it to go clanging across the floor a few feet. She turned in my direction, literally spat, then hiked her purse over her shoulder and stormed out the front door.

I turned back to look at Scott, unsure of what to say to him. He was shaking his head and walking toward the pile of overturned chairs that Josie had left in her wake. He started reaching down to right the chairs, and he glanced back at me with concern still filling his eyes.

"Are you sure you're all right?"

"I'm fine. A little shaken up, but fine." I didn't think he'd seen the pill bottle or noticed that I'd grabbed it. If he had, he didn't say anything about it. Instead, he continued shaking his head in disgust as he righted all of the overturned furniture.

"I can't believe that girl," he said. "She was acting like she was literally going to strangle you!"

I fingered at the pill bottle in my apron pocket. Perhaps, I thought, if she had strangled me, it wouldn't have been the first time that she'd killed someone. With shaking hands, I pulled the pill bottle out and held it up to show Scott. I needed his help, and I was hoping I was right in believing I could trust him.

He looked at the bottle in confusion. "What's that?"

I took a deep breath and explained it to him. I told him what Violet had told me about seeing Josie put ground up pills into Caitlin's drink, and then I told him that this had fallen out of Josie's purse just now. Scott turned pale as I explained everything.

"You should take that to the police. They'll want to analyze it and see what it is."

"I should," I said slowly. "But I'm not sure Mitch will believe me that this came from Josie. Maybe I should find a way to have it analyzed myself, and then I can confront Josie with it."

Scott frowned. "You're right to be wary of Mitch. And if you took in this bottle, he probably wouldn't trust you that it came from Josie. Tell you what. I know some of the guys in forensics. Let me take the bottle and ask them to analyze it. If it turns out to be something poisonous, I'll figure out a way to bring it up with Mitch. If Josie has poison, this probably isn't the only bottle of it she has. I'll convince Mitch to get a search warrant and go through all of Josie's things."

I nodded weakly. It wasn't the most ideal way to handle things, but I didn't see what choice I had. Mitch would listen to Scott more than he would listen to me. With any luck, Scott could convince Mitch to get a search warrant and go through Josie's things. I handed the bottle over to Scott.

"Here you go. Please keep me posted."

Scott nodded. "I will. Are you sure you're okay?"

"I'm fine." A lump formed in my throat. "Thank you for looking out for me. I have to say, even though this town frustrates me, it's nice to know that there are good people who see beyond the fact that I'm an outsider. You and Molly have both been so kind to me, even though I've been accused of murder."

Scott shrugged. "I like to think I can tell good people when I see them. And you're good people. Don't worry. I know this is all stressful right now, but I'm sure it will work out. In the end, the truth will come out. It always does." He smiled warmly at me, causing my stomach to flip-flop delightfully.

I smiled back weakly. "Thanks. And thanks for rescuing me from Josie. I owe you."

"If you really want to thank me, I wouldn't mind a complimentary slice of that peach brandy cobbler."

I grinned at him. "Easy enough. I'd trade a slice of peach brandy cobbler for my life any day."

I went to grab a plate, and put an extra large serving of cobbler on it for him. I set it on the counter, and Scott picked up the fork to start eating it without bothering to carry it to a table. After he'd taken his first bite, I reminded him that he'd said he had some news for me.

"What were you going to tell me before Josie stormed in here?" I asked.

"Oh! I almost forgot about that. It seemed like such a big deal, but I'll be honest: I'm not sure it's that exciting of news considering that Josie just tried to strangle you. I was going to tell you that I overheard down at the station that Todd is missing."

"Todd is missing? That seems like a pretty big piece of news to me."

"Yeah, I suppose so. I overheard Mitch talking about how they tried to contact Todd and haven't been able to reach him. He left the hotel where he'd been staying, and he's not answering his cell phone or his home phone back in San Francisco. I thought it pointed to the fact that he might be guilty, but after the way Josie just acted, and after what you told me about the pills, it seems like she might be the more likely suspect. Still, I suppose it's significant when a murder suspect disappears."

I nodded slowly. This new bit of news had only deepened my confusion.

"Perhaps they were working together," I said. "Maybe they both wanted to kill Caitlin, and now that it's done and they're being faced with a murder investigation, they're turning on each other."

Scott shrugged. "Perhaps. But I feel like there are pieces of this puzzle we're missing. It doesn't all seem to fit together quite right if you ask me."

I sighed. "I have to agree with you. Do me a favor, and keep your ears open for anything else you might overhear at the Sheriff's office."

"Will do," Scott said with a grin. "You can pay me for the information with more slices of peach brandy cobbler. This stuff is so good that you could probably convince me to eat it even if I knew there was poison in it."

I groaned. "Don't say that."

Scott shrugged. "Just trying to lighten the mood. But seriously, I'll keep an ear open for you. For now, I need to get going. I have a few more deliveries to make today. Are you sure you're all right? I'm worried about leaving you here alone after what Josie just did."

"I'm fine. Don't worry about me. I doubt she'll be back today, and she's not going to catch me off guard like that again."

"Alright," Scott said, but then grabbed a napkin and pulled a pen from his pocket. He scribbled down his phone number and pushed the napkin toward me. "Here's my cell number. Call me anytime, day or night, if you think you're in trouble."

He winked at me, and this time I didn't try to fight it when that warm, delicious feeling of happiness filled me from the inside out.

"Thanks," I said. "Hopefully I won't need it."

"Hopefully not," he agreed.

But as he walked out and I slipped the napkin into my apron pocket, I had the sinking feeling that I might need to call for help sooner rather than later.

Chapter Ten

After I finished closing up the pie shop for the day, I decided to go pay a visit to Mitch. The last thing I wanted to do was be in the same room as that arrogant, corrupt man. But I figured I should let him know that I had to head to San Francisco the next day. I didn't want him to realize I was gone and think that I had left because I was trying to run away. As I made my way to the police station, I thought of Todd. Why had he run away?

What was he hiding? What was Josie hiding? What was Theo hiding?

There were so many things that didn't make sense to me, and I was beginning to feel the pressure to somehow make them make sense. Despite how unconcerned Grams seemed to be, my heart felt like it was constantly tightening up in my chest with worry. How long did I have before I started to really feel the effects of being falsely accused of murder?

I tried to remember what I could from my criminal procedure class in law school. But that class had been so long ago, and I honestly hadn't paid much attention to it. I'd known I wasn't interested in criminal law, so I'd learned barely enough to squeak by on the final exam. Even that much I had promptly forgotten as soon as the exam was over.

Like it or not, I was about to get a refresher in criminal law.

I felt my heart tightening in my chest even more as I drove into the parking lot of the police station. In addition to a couple of police cruisers, an expensive looking Mercedes was parked out front. I wondered who it belonged to, but I didn't have to wonder for long. As soon as I entered the station, I heard a laugh that unfortunately sounded all too familiar.

Theo. It was the same sneering laugh that I'd heard the night Molly and I carried out our ridiculous plan to convince him to confess. The more I thought about that night, the more embarrassed I was that I'd ever tried anything so foolish. Why on earth had I thought a man like Theo would be nervous or intimidated by Molly and me? I should have known that Theo would be well prepared to answer any challenges about the murder.

In a rush, I turned to leave the police station. I didn't particularly want to confront Theo again right now—especially not in front of Mitch, whom I was sure would take Theo's side in all of this. But before I could make my escape, Theo and Mitch appeared in the front room of the station.

"Well, well, well," the pompous Sheriff Mitchell said. "If it isn't one of our murder suspects come to pay me a visit, live and in person. Come to confess, did you? I must say, it would make my job a lot easier. Although honestly, half the fun of being a sheriff is putting pressure on criminals until they work themselves into a corner. If you're already confessing, then this game was over a bit too quickly."

I scowled at him. "I'm not here to confess. I didn't murder Caitlin, so you won't be getting a confession from me. Not today, not ever."

Mitch seemed amused by this. "We'll see about that," he snorted. "But if you're not here to confess yet, then to what do I owe the displeasure of seeing you?"

I cleared my throat uncomfortably, and glanced at Theo. He was looking at me with his mouth hanging open. Too late, I realized that until this moment, he hadn't realized that I was one of the suspects in the murder investigation. I could see the wheels turning in his head. After a few moments' pause, he burst out laughing.

Theo's face crinkled up into a grin that was maddeningly adorable. Why did all of the jerks always get all the good looks?

"You're a murder suspect in this case?" he asked. "No wonder you were so keen on trying to get me to confess to a murder I didn't commit. You were just looking for someone else to take the blame for your crime."

Theo laughed again, and I resisted the urge to strangle him in much the same way that Josie had strangled me an hour ago.

Mitch glanced back and forth between Theo and me, looking slightly confused.

"Wait a minute," the sheriff said. "I take it you two have met?"

"That we have," Theo said. "This young lady showed up on my doorstep in the middle of the night a few days ago, trying to get me to confess to Caitlin Dixon's murder."

I bristled. Ordinarily, I would quite enjoy being referred to as a young lady. I was at that stage of life where I could feel my youth slipping away, and anyone who treated me like I still had some youth left made me happy. But when Theo called me a young lady, it came across as patronizing.

"It wasn't exactly the middle of the night," I protested. "I just stopped by after leaving the police station, to let the real murderer know that I was onto him."

I crossed my arms, knowing full well that Theo wasn't going to admit to anything and that Mitch was going to support Theo. But still, I wanted Theo to know that I wasn't backing away from my theory. Sure, a few things today had given me reason to admit to the possibility that Josie or Todd might have been the ones who actually murdered Caitlin. But on the whole, Theo still seemed like the most likely suspect to me.

Mitch did not look amused. His usually sneering face had morphed into a more serious glare. "Miss James," he said, his voice sounding angrier and more serious than I'd ever heard it before. "I would advise you to leave the matter of this murder investigation to the police. We are professionals, and this is a situation best dealt with by professionals. Not only that, but I don't think someone suspected of murder herself should be prancing around accusing other people."

I wanted to tell him that someone falsely suspected of murder had every right to be prancing around accusing other people, especially when those other people were much likelier to have committed the murder then I was. But at that moment, I just wanted to get out of the police station and away from Theo and Mitch.

So I ignored Mitch's comment and plunged forward with the reason I had come here in the first place. It wouldn't have been my first choice to explain to Mitch in front of Theo that I had to leave town, but I was completely done with the day. I just wanted to take care of business and get out of there.

"Well, Mitch, I didn't come here to accuse anyone else. I just came to let you know that I'll need to be in San Francisco tomorrow. But don't worry. I'll be back by the evening. I just wouldn't want you to think I was doing something suspicious like disappearing completely, as I've heard one of the other murder suspects has done."

From the surprise on Mitch's face when I made that last remark, I got the feeling that it wasn't common knowledge that Todd was missing, and that he wasn't happy that I knew. But he smoothed over his surprised expression quickly, and scowled at me instead.

"And what exactly is so important in San Francisco that it can't wait until after this murder investigation is over? I don't like my suspects leaving town on me."

"Well, frankly, I don't care very much what you like or don't like. As long as I'm here for my court date, what does it matter? And as it happens, I have another court date that I need to attend to in San Francisco. It's a domestic matter, completely unrelated to anything here, but I need to attend."

Mitch was frowning at me, but Theo somehow caught on quickly. He laughed.

"What's the matter?" Theo asked between chuckles. "You had a husband and then he decided he didn't want to be married to a murderer anymore, so he divorced you?"

I felt smoke coming out of my ears. Mitch still looked slightly confused, but I figured Theo would be happy enough to explain everything to him. I rolled my eyes for good measure, then turned on my heel and left the police station.

When I got to my car, my hands were shaking as badly as Violet's usually did. I didn't know why exactly I was so angry. Why did it matter to me what Mitch or Theo thought of me? I supposed that knowing that two of the most influential men in Sunshine Springs were laughing at me was what put me in a foul mood. All I had wanted to do was come to a new town and start over. But instead of being accepted as the smart, kind, talented baker that I was, I was being treated like an outsider, a murderer, and a laughingstock. At least Scott and Molly seemed to still be willing to be my friends.

I got into my car and put my hands on the steering wheel, willing them to stop shaking. I wished Molly didn't have so many events at the library this week. I could have used a friend who could go out for drinks with me. The only other person I could go get a drink with in Sunshine Springs was Grams, and I wasn't sure I wanted to hang out with Grams right now. If she told me one more time that I was blowing things out of proportion, I might lose it on her.

Unfortunately, I had to at least see Grams for a few moments to pick up Sprinkles. But I planned to make that as quick as I could, running in to get the dog and telling Grams I had to leave right away because I was tired and had a long drive to San Francisco the next morning. Grams had told me to leave Sprinkles with her while I went to San Francisco, but I wanted to take him. I didn't want to be alone when my divorce finalized. But I didn't tell this to Grams, because I was afraid she would think I was weak and playing the victim. Instead, I told her that Sprinkles would love a chance to go down and see the city he'd grown up in.

I'd have to pay someone to watch him while I was actually in the courthouse. Somehow, I didn't think the judge in my divorce proceedings would appreciate a large Dalmatian sitting by my side in the courtroom while my marriage officially ended. But at least Sprinkles would be there when I came out as an officially single woman.

Taking a deep breath, I did my best to steady my hands as I turned the engine on in my worn down car. If I could get my business going well enough here in Sunshine Springs, one of the first things I was going to splurge on was a new car. Oh sure, this little car had been faithful to me for over a hundred thousand miles. I couldn't complain about that. But it was getting too old to be trustworthy, especially since I was no mechanic and didn't have the faintest idea how to fix anything that might go wrong. That had been fine when I lived in the city and could take public transportation anywhere I needed to go. But here in Sunshine Springs, it was difficult to even get a taxi. Of course, the way things were going right now, maybe I wouldn't even need a car. Maybe I'd be spending all my time in a jail cell.

I frowned and chewed my lower lip as I started to pull out of the parking lot. I couldn't think like that. I couldn't give up hope. I was innocent, and I wasn't going to let the true murderer get away with killing Caitlin Dixon. I just had to focus and keep looking. There was an explanation for all of this—an explanation that didn't involve me—and I was going to find it.

As I started down the road that ran behind the police station, I saw a trio of dark figures standing in the shadows. I slowed my car, and tried to appear as though I wasn't looking in their direction. It wasn't dark yet, so I didn't have my headlights on. But a car driving down this road was still pretty obvious. It wasn't a well-traveled road, and the only reason I took it was because it was the fastest way to get to Grams' house.

Thankfully, the three figures behind the police station seemed too engrossed in whatever they were talking about to notice a car driving by. I strained my eyes to see them, and I quickly realized that the three men were Theo, Mitch, and the Sunshine Springs Mayor. Whatever they were discussing must have required some serious focus. They were huddled together, and it looked like they were looking over a notebook or tablet.

My heart froze in my chest. Was Theo discussing pilfering money from the city with the Mayor? And was Mitch in on this? I shouldn't have been surprised. If Theo and the Mayor were doing something shady in the city, then they would have to pay Mitch off. Otherwise, the sheriff would have been able to arrest them both.

For the first time since I arrived at the station, I realized that it was a bit strange that Theo had been there. It was clear from the way that he was happily talking and laughing that he hadn't been there because Mitch was arresting him or questioning him regarding Caitlin's murder. Had he been there to discuss whatever side deal these men all had going on to line their pockets with the city's money?

As I drove slowly by, Theo looked up and looked straight toward my car. I felt my blood run cold, and I told myself to look quickly away as though I had seen nothing. For some reason, going to Theo's house that night with Molly had been easy enough to do. But letting Theo know that I'd just caught him right in the act of something shady terrified me. If he was a murderer, and he thought I had evidence against him, was he going to murder me, too?

But despite my sudden fear, I couldn't quite manage to look away. It was like when you drove by a car wreck, and you told yourself not to be the idiot rubbernecking and slowing down traffic, but you couldn't help gaping at the destruction anyway.

I was gaping at the destruction here. But the scary thing was, it was my life that was being destroyed. It didn't matter how much Violet vouched for Theo's character. Violet was a crazy, delusional old woman who had no idea what she was talking about. It was clear to me that these three men were in on some sort of scheme together—some sort of illegal scheme that had driven them to murder.

A murder that they were going to let me take the fall for.

Theo, as I was learning was his way, seemed amused by the fact that I was staring at him. A sneering smile crossed his face, and he raised his hand to give me a small wave. Abruptly, I turned my gaze away and sped off down the road toward Grams' house. I was glad that I had a good excuse to escape to San Francisco tomorrow, and I wondered whether I could get away with skipping bail and never coming back.

As the police station faded from view in my rearview mirror, my hands started shaking once again.

Chapter Eleven

The next morning, I woke up bright and early before the sun itself had even woken up. I quickly grabbed my briefcase full of important paperwork pertaining to the divorce, and slipped into the skirt suit I had set out the night before. I once again looked like a professional, high-powered lawyer, but these days my skirt suit felt more like a costume then like the second skin it used to be.

I was okay with that. I'd never enjoyed being a lawyer all that much, and if today was the last time in my life that I had to go into a courthouse, I'd be more than fine with that. Of course, if I wanted today to be the last time I was ever in a courthouse, I still had to figure out who had murdered Caitlin Dixon. But that would have to wait until tomorrow. I had plenty of other things to worry about today.

"Come on, Sprinkles," I said as I grabbed my car keys and headed toward the door. "Let's go get this over with."

Sprinkles stood reluctantly, stretched, and ambled after me with his tail lazily wagging as though we were about to head out to spend a happy day at the beach or the park. Oh to be a dog, I thought. Oh to be able to enjoy life for its simple joys, and to not constantly feel like the weight of the world was crushing you down.

Sprinkles bounded out the front door ahead of me, finding a sudden rush of energy as the fresh air hit his face. I couldn't help but laugh as the black and white spotted blur rushed past me.

"Hold on, Sprinkles!" I quickly turned to lock the door on my small, cozy cottage. "I don't know where you think we're going, but this trip isn't going to be as exciting as you seem to think it is right now."

In response, Sprinkles barked loudly. I winced and turned to hush him. The last thing I needed was for him to wake up my neighbors. They were all already looking for reasons to complain about me, so I'm sure they would happily whine about being woken up by my unruly Dalmatian in the early dawn hours. Worse, though, was that if they saw me leaving this early, their tongues would start wagging about where I was going. I'm sure it wouldn't be too long before someone talked to Theo or Mitch and heard the news that I was heading into San Francisco for divorce proceedings. It wasn't like this was some great secret I needed to keep. It's just that it wasn't my favorite topic of conversation, and I didn't want to be forced to discuss it ad nauseam with a bunch of busybodies who were only interested in my life because it provided good gossip fodder.

Sprinkles ignored me and barked again. With a sigh, I jiggled the doorknob to make sure it was locked before turning to reprimand Sprinkles. But then I saw why he was barking, and my eyes widened.

Molly was standing in my front yard, holding two to-go cups of coffee and what looked like a box of donuts. Her little red sports car was parked on the street right in front of my house. Sprinkles had spotted her, and had run up to her excitedly. He was dancing around her now, barking and begging to be petted. But Molly couldn't very well pet him when her hands were full of coffee and doughnuts.

"Down, Sprinkles," she said with a laugh. "Down, boy! I'm happy to see you too, but my hands are little bit full at the moment. I promise as soon as I set this stuff down, I'll give you a proper backrub. I might even sneak you a donut, if I can find a moment where your mama isn't watching me like a hawk."

Sprinkles whined happily and sat down on the grass in front of Molly, his tail swishing around faster than a helicopter propeller.

I was confused. "Molly? What are you doing here?"

She held up the coffee and donuts. "I brought you some breakfast. I would have brought you some pie from the best pie shop in town, but it appears they're closed today."

"Yeah, well, I'm going to—"

"San Francisco," she finished for me. "I know. I overheard your grandma talking about it at the library yesterday afternoon. She was complaining that you had to go to the big city, but that you refused to leave Sprinkles here because you didn't want to go alone."

I groaned. I guess Grams saw right through my attempt at pretending that bringing Sprinkles along had nothing to do with the fact that I wasn't too excited about facing the divorce proceedings alone.

"Yeah. I have some, um, business to take care of in the city. But I should be back by tonight. Are you still busy at the library? If you're not, then I'd love to go out for drinks with you."

Molly smiled kindly at me. "Izzy, your grandma told me why you're going to the city."

I felt my blood starting to boil. "Why would she do that? She shouldn't be running around town, blabbing to everyone about my business."

"She wasn't blabbing to everyone. She told me in confidence, because I asked her why you were going. And because she's worried about you. She doesn't want you to face this alone, but she doesn't think you'll let her go with you. She thought that if she told me what was going on, that I might step up and make the trip with you. And she was right."

My jaw dropped. "But I thought you were super busy at the library this week. Besides, you haven't known me very long. Why would you want to come to the city with me for such an unhappy affair? I'm sure you have better things to do with your day."

"Better things to do than to be there for a friend? I think not. I've already taken the day off work. I explained to the junior librarians that it was an emergency. Don't worry, they've got everything covered, and it will actually be good for them to take care of all of this by themselves. Sometimes I think that they need a bit more experience dealing with things on their own, so that I don't always have to be there babysitting them. Now, come on. Get in my car. I'm driving."

"But…" I tried again.

Molly shook her head at me. "No buts about it. You shouldn't have to deal with the stress of driving into the city on a day that's already so stressful. You just relax in the passenger seat, and let me at least take care of the driving part of today."

I opened my mouth to protest again, but Sprinkles was already running toward Molly's car. He took a flying leap toward her open driver's side window, and he managed to get his head and front paws in. But the rest of his body hung awkwardly from the window. I winced when he pushed his paws against the red paint on her door as he not so gracefully wiggled into the car.

"Sprinkles! You're going to ruin the paint on Molly's car."

Molly laughed. "Don't worry about it. He wasn't scratching that hard."

She walked toward the car, and I shrugged and reluctantly followed. It didn't look like Molly or Sprinkles were going to let me argue about this. A few minutes later, we were on the highway heading toward San Francisco, munching on donuts and downing coffee. Molly kept the mood light, laughing as she told me stories about the adorable children who had been attending the book fair at the library this week. Sprinkles had assumed his usual spot, sitting in the backseat with his head poking into the front seat between Molly and me. He managed to steal a donut or two, and for once I didn't fight him about it. Today was going to be a long day. I knew I shouldn't let him eat donuts, but I couldn't find it in my heart to begrudge him a little bit of sugar.

As the sun rose higher into the sky, bathing the world in a brilliant orange-pink sunrise, I almost could have fooled myself into thinking that I was heading off for a fun girls' weekend in San Francisco. My heart ached with gratitude toward Molly. She'd only known me about a week, and she was already being a better friend to me than most of my friends in San Francisco. Those friends had known me for years and yet had disappeared as soon as everything with the divorce started going down. Perhaps this was the sort of small town friendship I'd heard so much about. I'd moved to Sunshine Springs because I wanted to belong and be part of a community. Molly was treating me like I belonged, and no matter how things turned out over the next few weeks or months, I would be forever grateful to her for that.

But reality hit me hard when she dropped me off in front of the courthouse. I promised to call her as soon as I was done, and she promised not to go far. She told me she would park somewhere and go for a walk with Sprinkles, assuring me that she was always excited to see a new part of the city. Thankful for her, and for the fact that I wouldn't have to pay someone to watch Sprinkles since she was here, I headed into the courthouse. I was early, and as I sat and waited for my assigned time to go before the judge, my mind wandered off into all kinds of horrible scenarios of what it would be like to step into a courtroom and face murder charges.

My mood did not improve when my ex-husband appeared. He tried to act like this was all some sort of mutually agreed-upon situation. But it was anything but mutual. I hadn't asked for him to run off and cheat on me, forcing me to lose all of my friends. Although I was grateful for the chance to start over in Sunshine Springs, I would have rather started over under different circumstances. Besides, it remained to be seen whether my attempt at starting over was going to work out.

I did my best to speak as little as humanly possible to him and to his lawyer. I didn't have a lawyer. I was acting as my own lawyer, even though I wasn't a family law attorney. I hadn't wanted to dip into my savings even more to pay someone to do what I'd decided I could figure out how to do for myself.

Thankfully, the whole ordeal didn't take too long. The judge quickly approved our divorce settlement, and I watched numbly as a bored-looking law clerk took a rubber stamp with the date and the word "Filed" on it and pounded it across each copy of the divorce settlement, stamping away my former life as she did.

I called Molly, feeling surprisingly at peace. I was just glad to have this all done. Molly had been walking not far from the courthouse, and she swung by on foot to pick me up so that we could walk back to her car together. She gave me a big hug when I emerged from the courthouse.

"It's over," she said simply, squeezing one of my hands as she did. "What do you say we go have some ice-cream to celebrate your newfound freedom?"

I nodded. "Okay."

I wasn't sure whether I could actually eat anything right now, but I wanted a few moments to decompress before getting back in the car for the long drive back to Sunshine Springs.

Sprinkles stuck close to my side as we walked, hovering protectively as though he understood I needed extra comfort right now. We hadn't gone very far when he suddenly started growling.

Perhaps he was being a little bit too protective.

"Sprinkles!" I said. "Calm down. You grew up in the city. You should be used to this. Why are you so unsettled by crowds all of a sudden?"

Sprinkles ignored me, and continued growling. Then, suddenly, he jerked forward on his leash and started trying to run.

"Sprinkles!" I shouted as I jerked the leash back. "What on earth has gotten into you?"

Sprinkles ignored me and continued trying to run forward. I looked over at Molly, feeling embarrassed that my normally well-trained dog was acting like this. He wasn't putting on a very good show today. But Molly wasn't looking at Sprinkles. She was looking somewhere beyond him, up on the sidewalk ahead.

"Izzy! It's Todd!"

I looked where her finger was pointing, and saw that she was right. Up ahead of us, Todd the photographer was walking quickly down the street, coming right toward us. He wore a baggy pair of jeans and an old T-shirt. His hair was disheveled, and even from here I could see the bags under his eyes. He had his large camera slung over one shoulder, and on the other shoulder he carried a canvas messenger bag that wasn't closed properly. He looked like a total mess.

No wonder, I thought. I'm sure murdering someone and then skipping town to escape your court date would take its toll on anyone.

He seemed lost in thought, and hadn't seen us yet. But a moment later, Sprinkles' growls turned into an all-out barking fit. Startled by the sound, Todd looked over. When he saw Sprinkles, his brow furrowed with worry. Then his eyes moved past Sprinkles to look at first me, and then Molly. A shocked expression crossed his face as he recognized us, and a split-second later he turned around and started running as fast as he could, his messenger bag and camera flapping wildly behind him.

Molly had already started running. "Those are the actions of a guilty man if you ask me!" she yelled, although I barely understood her over Sprinkles' barking.

I let go of Sprinkles' leash so that he could run after Todd. All around me, shocked faces of passersby stared as they saw a disheveled man being chased by a woman in yoga pants, a barking Dalmatian, and a woman in a skirt suit. What a sight we must have made.

But I didn't have time to think about how ridiculous I must look. Todd was getting away, and Molly was right: he was acting awfully guilty.

"Stop that man!" I yelled at the shocked bystanders. "Stop him now! He's a murderer!"

Chapter Twelve

The next minute or two sped by in a blur. Molly and Sprinkles were much faster than I was. I tried to keep up, but running in a skirt suit wasn't easy.

Unfortunately, none of the bystanders seemed interested in getting involved. Maybe they thought we were crazy, and that Todd wasn't really a murderer. Or maybe they believed us that he was a murderer, and they figured it was better to stay far away from someone who was capable of killing. Whatever the case, Todd was proving to be much better at weaving through the crowds than Molly or Sprinkles. Sprinkles seemed to be slowly gaining on him, but in the end it wasn't enough. I watched as Todd hailed a taxicab.

"Stop!" I yelled, as though my words might actually do something to keep him from getting away.

"I'm not stopping!" he yelled back. "I'm not going back to that god-awful town! I'm not going to let my life be ruined by some crazy old Sunshine Springs local!" With that, he disappeared into the taxi, and the taxi sped away.

I stopped, feeling dejected as I desperately tried to catch my breath. I hoped to God that my now-official ex-husband had gone the other way when he left the courthouse. I didn't want to think about the humiliation I would feel if he'd seen me running down the streets yelling like a madwoman. And I definitely didn't want to think about the humiliation I would feel if he discovered that I had kicked off my new life in Sunshine Springs by managing to get accused of murder.

Luckily, my ex was nowhere to be seen. I hobbled toward Molly, contemplating whether the risk of putting my bare feet directly on the dirty sidewalk was worth it to take off my dress shoes. I decided I would rather stay on the safe side and avoid some sort of horrible foot infection. I kept my uncomfortable shoes on, at least for the moment.

As I approached Molly, she looked just as dejected as I felt. Sprinkles was a few feet away, barking incessantly and spinning in small circles. The crowds of people walking down the sidewalk parted ways around him, giving him a wide berth. Many of them were muttering about irresponsible pet owners who couldn't keep their dogs under control.

"Sprinkles!" I pleaded. "Please stop barking and come here. He got away in a taxi. There's nothing we can do about it."

Sprinkles ignored me, and kept barking. With a frustrated sigh, I decided I was going to have to go get him physically. I marched toward him, on the verge of losing my temper. But when I reached him, I realized that a folder of papers and photographs had fallen on the street and scattered around him. I immediately recognized some of the photographs as being taken at the Sunshine Springs Winery's tasting room.

I bent down and picked up a few of the papers. Some of them looked like printed out account ledgers, some looked like printed out emails, and a few others were handwritten notes on sheets of notebook paper. After just a few moments of shuffling through the mess, I realized that I was looking at a whole pile of evidence. I wasn't sure whether this evidence was all just about the winery scandal, or whether some of it had to do with the murder. Either way, I felt my excitement growing. Perhaps there was something in here that would prove helpful to me.

"Good boy, Sprinkles," I said patting his head. "Sorry I yelled at you when you were just trying to tell me this was here."

Sprinkles, not one to hold a grudge, licked my hand happily and twirled around in circles a few times, evidently quite pleased with himself.

By this time, Molly had arrived next to me. She must have realized, as I had, that we were looking at some sort of evidence.

"Todd must have dropped this," she said. "I wonder if there's something in here that proves he killed Caitlin."

"Maybe," I said slowly. "Or maybe this is evidence he's gathered trying to prove who the true murderer was. It looks like there's a lot in here about Theo's winery. And did you hear him yell about how he's not going to have his life ruined for some Sunshine Springs local?"

"Yeah." Molly frowned. "That struck me as a little bit weird. Caitlin wasn't local, so he wasn't referring to having his life ruined over her or her murder. Maybe he was talking about Theo."

I started quickly making a neat pile out of all of the papers and photographs. I felt my heart starting to pound with hope and excitement. "Maybe there's something in here—something Todd found—that will incriminate Theo. Maybe Todd is innocent, and he got so frustrated with the whole thing that he ran. I have to admit that I've been tempted to run a few times myself. It's pretty disconcerting to walk around in a town where everyone knows you're accused of murder, and where you worry constantly that you might be unfairly put in jail."

Molly stood above me, looking down with a hand on her hip. "Don't you dare run. I know you didn't commit this murder, and we're going to find a way to prove it. Not only that, but I'm pretty sure that most of the other folks in town also know that you didn't do it. If they really thought you'd poisoned someone, do you think they'd eat the pie at your café? Your grandma's right, you know? Everyone looks at this as some sort of hazing ritual by Mitch. They're not taking it seriously."

I frowned as I stood with the folder. "Well, I hope everyone is amused by this, then. Because it sure feels serious to me."

Molly looked at me with sympathy in her eyes. "I know it's stressful. But really, don't worry. We'll get this figured out. And I have a feeling that everything in this folder is going to help us. Let's head back to my car. I'll drive us back toward Sunshine Springs, and you can start sorting this all out on the way."

I nodded as I started to follow her, the weight of the folder heavy and promising in my hands. Had Todd just accidentally given me the key to my freedom, and to clearing my name? I was about to find out.

My heart pounded hopefully in my chest. I couldn't wait to start going through these papers.

Chapter Thirteen

Traffic out of San Francisco was horrendous, thanks to a multiple vehicle wreck. What should have been less than a two hour drive quickly turned into a three hour drive. Normally, I would have been beyond frustrated by this. But I hardly noticed the time passing as I sat in Molly's passenger seat and pored over the papers and photographs.

Everything was completely disorganized, and getting it all into some semblance of order took up a good portion of the ride back to Sunshine Springs. I wasn't sure whether the papers had been messed up because they fell out of the folder, or whether Todd had had them this disorganized in the first place. One thing, however, was clear: Todd had been gathering evidence about the scandal that Caitlin had been investigating before she died. The most obvious reason for him to be doing this was that he also thought Theo had murdered Caitlin. And if Todd was trying to solve the murder too, then he must be innocent as well.

Now I really wished that we'd caught up with him. If he was working on the same case with the same idea of bringing Theo down, then perhaps we could have worked together and gotten this solved quicker. I didn't blame him for not trusting me, though. After all, I'd been running after him while calling him a murderer. And if he had been wrongfully accused, I knew just how he felt. I myself felt indignant and reluctant to trust anyone, especially when it seemed that law enforcement in Sunshine Springs was conveniently in Theo's back pocket.

Unfortunately, I doubted we were going to be able to get a hold of Todd. He must be hiding out somewhere, and I'm sure he wasn't answering his phone. I was also sure he was going to be livid when he realized his folder of evidence was missing. What had he been planning to do with it? Was he on his way to a coffee shop to review it? Or had he been heading toward the courthouse with plans to show it to someone there? Perhaps he'd been in contact with a lawyer, or someone from law enforcement in San Francisco. I had so many questions for Todd, but I wasn't likely to get answers from him anytime soon. My only hope was that if he was innocent and realized that we now had all of his evidence, or at least a good chunk of his evidence, that he'd be forced to contact us in an attempt to get it back.

In the meantime, I was going to learn as much as I could from this folder of goodies that had fallen into our hands.

"There are a lot of accounting records in here," I said as Molly guided her little sports car down the highway. Traffic had finally cleared up, and we were humming along at a nice pace now.

"Does any of it look suspicious?" Molly asked.

"I don't know. It's quite a mess. It looks like records from both the city and from the winery, but quite honestly nothing in the winery records looks off. There appear to be funds leaving the city's coffers for no reason, but I don't see those same funds showing up in the winery's records."

"Maybe Theo didn't record those amounts. It would've made sense to try to hide them instead, don't you think? If he was stealing money from the city, it's not like he'd want to make a record of that for anyone to find."

I nodded. "Right. Well, that's just my first impression. There are a lot of records here. It's not just the accounting records. It looks like there are emails between someone from the City Council and someone else on the outside, but I have no idea who because the email addresses are all blacked out."

"Do you think Todd found all of this? Or were these Caitlin's notes on the scandal?"

"I think these were Caitlin's notes. There are a lot of handwritten notes all over these papers, and it looks like girly handwriting. No matter who wrote the notes, though, they're worth going through. There's a lot here to unpack. I think we should get together tonight. Maybe have some dinner, and start going through it all in some sort of methodical manner? That is, if you have time tonight."

I felt my cheeks heat up with embarrassment. Who was I to ask Molly for more time? I knew she was busy. She'd already taken the whole day to come to San Francisco with me. Maybe she didn't have time to spend the evening going over boring accounting records.

But Molly was looking at me like I was crazy. "Are you kidding me? I can't think of anything more important right now than going through these records and figuring out a way to prove that you aren't a murderer."

I looked over at her and smiled gratefully. She looked at me for a brief moment and smiled back before turning her eyes back to the road.

"What did I do to deserve a friend like you?" I asked.

Molly threw back her head and laughed. "Well, for one thing, you make such a good banana cream pie that it's not even fair. I knew I had to become good friends with you so I could get first dibs on all your pies. But also, I love a good adventure. And even though I know this adventure has been quite stressful for you, it *has* been an adventure. How many times in my life will I have the chance to help chase down a murderer?"

"You know, some people might be just fine going their whole lives without having to track down a murderer."

"Well, that's a pretty boring life if you ask me!"

I grinned. "In a couple decades, you're going to take my grandma's place as the craziest old lady in Sunshine Springs."

Molly's smile widened. "That's a place I would take with pride. Your grandma is one of Sunshine Springs' best citizens. I know sometimes it seems like she's hard on you, but she loves you more than anything. She talks about you all the time. She did even before you moved here. I know she has her own way of showing that she cares, but she does care. You know that, right?"

I sighed. "I know. And I love her more than anything, too. It's just so frustrating sometimes that she can't seem to take anything seriously. Not even a murder accusation."

"Don't worry. If it gets to the point that it needs to be taken seriously, she will. But in the meantime, I think she knows that you're a big girl, and you're more than capable of handling this on your own."

"Well, not entirely on my own. I've got your help, and I'm grateful for that. In fact, to show you I'm grateful, why don't we go to the pie shop to sort through all of this? I have a few pies left over from yesterday that I didn't sell, and we can munch on them while we work. They'll be a day old, so they're not as fresh as what I normally sell in the store. But they'll still be really good."

"You don't have to ask me twice. I'm sure even one of your day-old pies tastes better than any of the other pies I could find anywhere in Sunshine Springs. I'll need to swing by the library for an hour or so to take care of a few things. Maybe you could go and start sorting the papers, and I'll catch up to you at the café as soon as I can?"

I nodded. "That sounds good." I chewed my lower lip thoughtfully for a few moments. "Do you think that perhaps we should ask Scott to come help us?"

Molly glanced over at me and raised an eyebrow. "Scott the delivery guy?"

"Yeah. He's been keeping an ear out for me while he does deliveries to see if he might hear anything useful to my case. And he *did* save me yesterday night when Josie came into the store and attacked me."

Molly looked over at me and her eyes widened until they must have been about twice their normal size. "Wait a minute. Josie attacked you? You never told me that!"

I winced. "Yeah. She attacked me. It wasn't a big deal, really. She just caught me off guard, and Scott stepped in to pull her off of me. I guess I didn't say anything because I was so preoccupied with the divorce proceedings this morning that I didn't really want to talk about the murder case. And then on the drive home I've been so interested in all these papers. Actually, I have a few other things to tell you. Like the fact that Violet thinks that Josie is the one who poisoned Caitlin, and there's possibly some evidence that that's true."

Molly glanced over at me and raised an eyebrow. "You do have a lot to tell me."

"Yeah, I do. I haven't even mentioned yet how I saw Theo, Sheriff Mitch and the Mayor having a secret little meeting yesterday evening."

"What?" Molly exclaimed. "You've been holding out on me!"

"Not on purpose," I insisted. "Tell you what: why don't you go finish up everything you need to do at the library. I'll go to the pie shop and start organizing these papers. I'm not opening at all today, since I didn't have time to bake pies this morning. I'll call Scott and ask him to meet us there as well, and when you both get there I'll tell you both everything I know. Then we'll all be on the same page regarding Theo, Josie, and Todd."

"Alright. But it's going to be torture waiting even an hour to hear all of this." Molly sighed. "I do have to get a few things done, but I have a feeling I'm going to be working quicker than I ever have before."

I took a deep breath. "Good. And then, when you get to the pie shop, you can help me work through all of these papers as quickly as possible. I don't know why, but I have this uneasy feeling that I'm running out of time."

Molly nodded grimly and clutched the steering wheel tighter as she crossed into Sunshine Springs' city limits. I noticed her knuckles turning white. "I think you're right," she said. "But don't worry. We'll figure this out. We'll clear your name and find the real killer before it's too late."

I hoped she was right. After the confrontation I'd had with Josie last night, I couldn't stop thinking about how the real killer was on the loose, and might easily kill again if they weren't stopped soon.

I shivered, even though it was the middle of July.

Chapter Fourteen

Several hours later, Molly, Scott and I all sat inside the dimly lit Drunken Pie Café. I kept the front door locked and the lights low in hopes that no one would think I was open. I didn't have to worry too much about that, though. It was fairly late in the evening by this point, so the activity on Main Street was mostly dying down. Sunshine Springs wasn't much of a nightlife town, and the few bars and restaurants that catered to those who liked to stay out a bit later were all on the opposite side of the small downtown area. Besides that, it had started to rain. This was quite unusual for wine country in the middle of the summer, and many of the Sunshine Springs residents were hiding out at home tonight.

That was just fine by me. I didn't want to be bothered, and the rain fit my mood. I had a lot to figure out, and so far I hadn't had much luck. Before Scott and Molly arrived, I'd separated the papers into as organized of piles as I could manage. One pile held what looked like accounting statements from the winery, and another pile had accounting statements from the city. There were also hundreds of emails printed out. I was assuming the emails were mostly to and from the same person, but it was impossible to tell because the email addresses were all blacked out. I skimmed a few of the messages, and they seemed to be between a City Council member and someone outside the Council. This supported the idea that there was a scandal going on at the Sunshine Springs Winery, but nothing directly mentioned the winery. Not only that, but many of the emails that I did take time to read before Scott and Molly arrived appeared to be relatively benign.

But I figured there must be something good in there somewhere. Otherwise, why would Todd have been carrying them around? It just might take a while to get to the good stuff unless we were lucky. I put all of the emails in one pile, and figured we'd have to start going through them and hope for the best.

In another pile, I put all of the photographs. These must have been photos that Todd had taken during his brief stay in Sunshine Springs. I wasn't sure why he'd printed them all out. Nothing looked particularly out of the ordinary. There were photographs of Josie and Caitlin about town, and Todd had taken a few photos of them in the lobby of the hotel where they'd been staying. A few more photos showed them having breakfast at the Morning Brew Café, and then most of the other photos were of the winery.

It seemed Todd had documented every square inch of the place. Some of the photos that he'd taken of the grapevines were actually quite good. I chuckled, thinking that Theo should buy these from Todd to use in the winery's marketing. Too bad they were both accused of murder, and unlikely to be interested in any sort of business deal with each other.

Molly and I decided that it would be prudent to look carefully at each photo, even though they didn't seem to be anything special. Better safe than sorry. She and I would tackle the photos, carefully scrutinizing each one, while Scott started going through the account records. He'd offered to do that, saying that he'd helped his father out with accounts at his father's small auto body shop when he'd been younger.

I supposed I could have figured out the account records easily enough, but I wasn't going to complain about passing that job off to Scott. At least he could get the initial work of the first pass done and pull out anything that looked suspicious.

His job didn't turn out to be that hard: it didn't take him long at all to find something that looked suspicious. Like I had on the car ride over, he quickly identified spots in the city's accounting where money seemed to be missing, or where money had been designated for general funds which then had generic withdrawals that made no sense. I let him ponder on that while Molly and I continued to look at the photos.

"I don't think there's anything here," Molly said. "Todd took beautiful photos of the winery, that's for sure. But they don't show anything out of the ordinary. Just a bunch of tourists in the background, doing tastings just like Josie and Caitlin. Well, a bunch of tourists along with Violet. I guess she wasn't kidding when she told you she liked to hang out there."

I looked at a photo that Molly handed to me. Violet was indeed in the background, and I saw her staring down at Josie's purse. I shivered as I remembered Violet talking about Josie putting ground-up pills in Caitlin's wine. Had this photograph been taken before or after that moment had allegedly occurred? There was no way to know, except perhaps by asking Violet—and I wasn't ready to go talk to Violet about any of this yet. She'd made it pretty clear that she didn't approve of the fact that I was playing detective, so I'd save my questions for her until they were absolutely necessary.

I turned my attention to Josie's and Caitlin's smiles in the photo. Caitlin flashed her perfect white teeth at the camera, and her tanned skin seemed to glow in the light of the tasting room's chandeliers. I shook my head as I looked at the picture—one of the last pictures ever taken of Caitlin.

"Crazy, isn't it?" I asked. "She had no idea that just a few hours later she'd be dead."

Molly shook her head sadly. "Just goes to show that you can't take a single moment for granted."

We were quiet for a few moments, contemplating the brevity of Caitlin's life. Then, from a few tables away, Scott broke the silence with a long, exasperated sigh. Molly and I both looked up at him.

"What's wrong?" I asked.

He leaned back in his chair and ran his fingers through his hair. "It's just that I can't find anything in the winery's accounting records here to indicate a scandal. Everything looks squeaky clean on the winery's end."

"Is it possible it's in some other records that we don't have here?" I asked.

"It's possible. But that doesn't help us much right now. All we've established is that someone on city Council was definitely doing something shady. Or at least someone with access to the city's money. But we haven't tied it to the winery at all."

I frowned, and thought of the Mayor's meeting with Theo and Mitch last night. "There must be a tie somewhere. We'll just have to keep looking."

Molly set down the pictures she'd been looking at. "Are we sure it's the winery? Maybe we really are barking up the wrong tree.

Maybe the city's money is going to someone else in town, and Theo doesn't have anything to do with it."

I considered this. "But if Theo doesn't have anything to do with it, why did Caitlin end up poisoned? You'd think that whoever's involved in this deal would have been happy that she was going after the wrong person."

"Well, the other business owner who's getting the kickbacks from the city might have been happy about it. But it seems Caitlin was still onto the fact that someone on the City Council was illegally pilfering money. Maybe that person got nervous and thought Caitlin would destroy whatever little scheme they had going on. Maybe we've been looking in the wrong place all along, and it was actually someone from the City Council that poisoned Caitlin."

I stood up and started pacing, feeling frustrated. I felt like every time I thought we were getting close to the answer, we reached another dead end. Rather than narrowing down our list of suspects and closing in on the true killer, our field of suspects seemed to be only expanding. Was I going to need to add every single person from the Sunshine Springs City Council to the list? Or worse, was I going to need to add every single person that might have access to the city's coffers to the list?

Sprinkles seemed concerned about my pacing. He stood, and came over to nudge my hand with his warm muzzle. He'd been extra protective of me today. I wasn't sure whether it was because he somehow understood why I'd been in San Francisco this morning, and knew that I needed the extra love now that my divorce was finalized, or whether it was because of the commotion of chasing down Todd. Or perhaps he'd somehow even sensed that I'd been a nervous wreck last night when I picked him up from Grams' after the confrontation with Josie—the confrontation that had been followed by a confrontation with Mitch at the police station.

I rubbed my forehead. What a stressful week it had been. I went to open another bottle of wine, and poured myself a generous glass. Then I helped myself to another slice of pie. Why not? I was willing to try anything right now that might help me relax.

"Yeah," Molly said slowly as she put the photographs back into a neat pile. "We've looked through all the photographs too, and there's nothing in here that looks suspicious. Perhaps we should move on to reading the emails."

88

"You're right," Scott said. "I wish all the addresses weren't blacked out, but maybe there'll be something in the actual bodies of the emails somewhere that will help us out."

"It's so weird that all of the addresses are blacked out," I said. "Do you think Caitlin did that, or do you think they came to her like that?"

"I'm sure they came to her like that," Scott said. "I don't know what reason she possibly could have had to black out the addresses. It's not like she was trying to protect someone."

I nodded, and took a stack of emails. Scott and Molly each grabbed a stack as well, and for the next half hour, we all read in silence. Occasionally, I would come across an email that had a handwritten notation on it from Caitlin, but none of the notes were particularly helpful. Mostly, Caitlin had just written things like "this looks suspicious," or "check into this more later."

The emails themselves proved to be equally unhelpful. They all seemed to be between the same two people, but those two people were careful to never call each other by name or give any identifying information in the bodies of their emails. Most of the emails discussed things like upcoming community events in Sunshine Springs, or the general state of the wine business in the area. Now and then, references were made to amounts of money being transferred from the city's coffers to whomever was writing these emails. But the emails only mentioned the amounts of the transfers. That didn't give us any new information beyond what Scott had already found in the accounting records.

I was starting to get tired. It had been a long day, and the frustration of searching uselessly through all of this information was only making the day feel longer. Maybe Todd wasn't going to be all that angry that he'd lost these records, I thought ruefully. It didn't seem that there was much of use here.

But just as I was about to suggest that we call it a night, Scott suddenly let out a long, low whistle.

"Listen to this," he said. "I've got an email here talking about Caitlin and her investigation. Looks like one of our mystery correspondents realized that Caitlin was coming to Sunshine Springs to investigate things. They got a little nervous, and offered to pay off the other email correspondent if he or she would take care of Caitlin and make sure the investigation stopped."

Molly and I both looked up at Scott incredulously.

"Take care of Caitlin?" Molly finally asked. "You mean, murder her?"

"Well," Scott said. "They didn't exactly say to kill her or to murder her. They just said to take care of her. But I think the implication is pretty clear."

With my heart pounding, I stood and went to look over Scott's shoulder at the email. I felt sick to my stomach as I looked down at the letter and saw that Scott was right. Someone had definitely been hinting at the need to kill Caitlin off. Of course, we still had no idea who that someone was. But for the first time since Caitlin died, I was beginning to feel like we were at least on the right path here.

"Do you think we should show this to Mitch?" Molly asked. "I know he's not our favorite person at the moment, but he might be able to get a warrant to search the city's email servers and find out who sent these emails."

I considered for a moment. I wasn't keen on involving Mitch yet. I could just imagine him frowning at me for continuing to play detective after he'd told me not to, and I wasn't sure how I was going to explain to him where I'd gotten these emails from in the first place. I'd have to tell him the whole truth about running into Todd and then not immediately telling the Sunshine Springs Police Department about it. That was sure to make Mitch angry. But Molly was right. If we were going to find out who sent these emails, then we probably needed someone with access to the city's email servers. And none of us had that access, or knew how to get it.

"Yeah, you're right," I said reluctantly. "We should probably go ahead and tell Mitch about this. I suppose that means we'll have to tell him about the accounting records we found as well. I just wish we'd found something from the winery, too."

I was having a hard time getting used to the idea that Theo might not be guilty of anything. The guy seemed like such a jerk, and I'd been so convinced that he was the one in the wrong here. But so far, annoyingly, no evidence had come up to point directly toward him. In fact, since his winery records—at least the ones we had— looked pristine, it might be time to knock him off the suspect list. If he had nothing to hide, then he'd had no reason to poison Caitlin.

"Speaking of the Sheriff's Department," I said to Scott. "Have you heard any news about the bottle of pills we took from Josie?"

I'd meant to ask him about that earlier, and had been on the verge of doing so when I'd been interrupted with a question from Molly about whether either of us thought there was a way to track Todd down by contacting his coworkers at the San Francisco magazine where he'd worked.

I sighed. There were too many moving pieces in this murder investigation right now, and I was having trouble staying on top of everything.

"I haven't heard anything back about the pills," Scott said with a shrug. "I'll let you know as soon as I do. But for now, we still don't know whether she was carrying poison or just pain meds in her purse."

I nodded. "Okay. Well in that case, we should go ahead and call it a night. I'll go talk to Mitch in the morning about these emails. I was hoping I might have something to tell him about Josie as well, but I guess that will have to wait. I have a feeling now that Josie isn't the one we're looking for, anyway. I can't imagine that a City Councilmember would have been brazen enough to email Josie and tell her to take out her own sister. It must be someone else."

"You're right," Scott said. "I don't think Josie was the killer. Actually, I was thinking..."

But before Scott could finish telling us what he was thinking, we were all startled by the crashing of glass at the front door of the pie shop.

My heart jumped into my throat as I turned to see that the café's glass front door had been completely shattered.

Stepping over that shattered glass, crunching it beneath her feet with each step, Josie Dixon walked into my pie shop. She held a gun in her hand, and she raised it to point it right at my face.

"Nobody move unless you want me to blow you to pieces," she said as she took another crunching step toward us.

Chapter Fifteen

I'd heard people say that your entire life flashes before your eyes in life or death moments, but I'd always thought they were being a little bit dramatic. As I stood there staring down the barrel of Josie's gun, however, I realized that there was some truth to the statement. Flashes of memories raced across my mind, all the way from my childhood up to the present day. How was it possible that everything was going to end like this, on a rainy night in what was supposed to be a quiet, peaceful small town?

Scott was the first one to speak. "Josie, don't do something you'll regret. Lower the gun, and let's talk about this."

But his calm voice didn't seem to even register with her. She kept her gun trained on me, an angry snarl on her face.

Beside me, Sprinkles lowered his head and let out a long, low warning growl. *That* registered with Josie. She swung the gun downward to point it at my Dalmatian's head.

"No!" I shouted. In retrospect, shouting suddenly probably wasn't the best way to handle the situation. Josie jumped in surprise, and the gun went off. I screamed, expecting to see my beloved dog lying in a lifeless heap on the café floor. But Josie had jerked her arm when startled, and the bullet had lodged into the front counter of the café instead. Sprinkles was alive and well, and even angrier than he'd been a moment ago.

He growled, and started creeping toward Josie with his teeth bared.

"Sprinkles, no," I said. "Stay, please. For once in your life just listen to me, and stay where you are."

Amazingly, Sprinkles listened. He stopped creeping forward, but he did continue to growl.

My heart thumped in my chest, and I felt a cold sweat breaking out on my forehead. What was Josie going to do? Was she going to kill all of us right then and there? It seemed likely. If she was awful enough to kill her sister, then what would she care about three people who were practically strangers? I had a feeling we were done for, but I still had to try to save myself and my friends.

"Josie, I know you're upset. But there must be some way to resolve the situation other than killing the three of us. Let's talk about this."

Josie swung her gun back toward me, a wild look in her eyes. I got the feeling that she had never actually shot a gun before, because she seemed so distraught after accidentally firing it. She'd stared at the spot where the bullet lodged for quite some time, until my words seemed to bring her back to the present moment. Now I was worried that the next bullet she set off accidentally—or not so accidentally—was going to be in my direction.

"I don't want to talk to you," she said in a steely voice. "I only want back the papers you stole from Todd."

She glanced across the café tables for a moment, taking in the piles of photographs, account records, and emails that Scott, Molly and I had spent the evening reviewing.

My eyes widened. How had she known that Todd was missing the papers unless he'd told her? Were they working together? I'd been ready to admit Todd's innocence, thinking that there was no way someone guilty would have gone to such efforts to go through all of this information.

But perhaps he'd been hoarding the information to keep it from the cops.

Perhaps he and Josie had worked together to kill Caitlin in some kind of sick, twisted conspiracy.

Or perhaps Todd knew that Josie was guilty, and had been trying to protect her.

So many possibilities whirled through my mind, all in a split-second. In the end, all that mattered in that moment was getting out of this current situation alive. And no matter how useful all of these documents might be in proving my innocence, they were meaningless if my friends and I ended up shot and killed.

I raised my hands slowly above my head. "Okay, Josie. No worries. The documents are all yours. Take what you want, and then leave calmly."

Unsurprisingly, Molly and Scott seemed to agree that the best thing to do here was to give Josie what she wanted. They also raised their hands above their heads slowly, then backed away from the tables that were covered with papers.

Keeping a wary eye on us, Josie ran forward and began stuffing the papers into one of the large folders sitting nearby. She kept looking up at us nervously, as though at any moment we might change our minds, pounce on her, and try to take away the papers we'd just agreed to let her have. Every now and then, Josie waved the gun as if to remind us that she had the upper hand here.

Once all of the papers were more or less stuffed into the folder, Josie took the folder under her left arm and started backing away from us. With her right hand, she continued to point the gun at us, shaking it menacingly in our direction. I would have felt better if she would have just put the thing away, but she didn't seem inclined to do so. I guess I couldn't blame her. She probably thought that the moment she put it away, one of us would rush her and steal the papers back.

Perhaps she wasn't wrong about that. I could see the veins in Scott's forehead bulging, and I knew that it was all he could do right now to hold in his anger and frustration over the fact that we'd just lost all of this evidence. As for me, I was just relieved that it looked like I was going to get out of here alive. With each step backward that Josie took, I found myself breathing a little bit easier.

But just as I began to feel like the thousand ton weight of worry on my chest was lifting, Josie steadied the gun in my direction and laughed. Her laugh sounded crazy, almost like the laugh you'd expect from an overly-caricatured bad guy in some B movie.

"Did you really think I would just let all of you go? If it were up to you, I'd be going away to prison for life. It's bad enough my sister is gone, don't you think? I shouldn't have to have my life ruined as well."

"Josie!" I pleaded, and I'm ashamed to admit that my voice sounded downright hysterical.

But I was beginning to think that Josie really was crazy, and that she was going to kill us after all. None of what she was saying made any sense to me. I desperately wanted her to listen to reason, but her mind seemed like it was in a place far beyond logic right now. Still, I had to try.

"Killing us isn't going to bring your sister back, and it's definitely not going to keep you out of prison. Just put the gun down, and I'll help you in any way I can."

"You? Help me? Yeah, I don't buy into that for second. Nice try. Prepare to meet your maker."

I squeezed my eyes shut, hoping against hope that she was bluffing. My whole body tensed up, and I thought that it really was the end. But then, instead of the sound of a gunshot, the sound of shouting and broken glass crunching reached my ears. My eyes flew open just in time to see Mitch and Theo rushing through the broken front door of the pie shop to tackle Josie.

I winced, expecting Josie's gun to wildly go off again, but another gunshot never came. Somehow, Mitch or Theo had managed to get it out of her hand before she could react and send off another shot. I stared, openmouthed. Theo and Mitch rolled in the broken glass, trying to subdue Josie completely. She put up quite a fight— yelling and screaming, and insisting that she was not the one at fault here. I couldn't believe she was still trying to proclaim her innocence, but I guess I shouldn't have been surprised. After listening to everything that had come out of her mouth in the last few minutes, I thought that perhaps she was a good candidate for the insanity defense. She wasn't making any sense.

Beside me, Sprinkles was barking and growling. Every few moments he turned in an excited circle, as though he didn't know what to do with all of the anxious energy building up inside of him.

His noise and movements snapped me out of my shock.

"Sprinkles, calm down. It's okay. The police have her now."

Well, the police and Theo had her. I felt my cheeks redden with shame as I thought of how brashly I had accused Theo of being the murderer. Clearly, I'd been wrong about that. Tonight, he'd saved my life and helped subdue the true murderer. I owed him a bit of an apology.

The next several minutes went by in a blur. Mitch called for backup, and it didn't take long for the street in front of my pie shop to be filled with the flashing lights of police cruisers. As Mitch handed off Josie to one of his officers to take down to the station for questioning, I swallowed my pride and went to talk to Theo.

"I don't know how to thank you," I said. "I'd be dead right now if it wasn't for you. How did you know that we needed help?"

Theo grinned and shrugged. "I didn't. I just happened to be in the right place at the right time. Mitch and I were out for a stroll down Main Street, trying to snuff out some raccoons that have been causing trouble in the garbage bins. We thought that since it was late and rainy, and no one was out, that those rascals might be showing their faces. We were trying to catch them off guard. But it looks like we caught us much more than a raccoon tonight. Looks like we caught us a murderer."

"Looks like it," Molly said. It was the first thing she'd said since this whole ordeal had started, and her voice was even shakier than mine. I reached over and squeezed her hand.

"Don't worry. We're safe now, thanks to Theo." I turned back to look at him. "So you saw a crazy lady with a gun, and ran straight toward her? Pretty brave of you."

Theo laughed. "I do have my knight in shining armor moments. Gotta take them when you can." Then his face sobered. "Seriously, though. I didn't even think about it. I just reacted on instinct. Mitch and I both did. I can't believe she was brazen enough to come in here with a gun and threaten to kill all three of you. What were you all doing here? I thought the pie shop was closed today?"

I blushed a little, remembering that Theo had known that I was heading down to San Francisco for a divorce proceeding today. That divorce proceeding, and this morning, felt like it had been a thousand years ago. I rubbed my forehead.

"Well, it's kind of a long story. When I was in the city today, I ran into Todd."

"Todd?" Theo exclaimed. "The same Todd who went missing in the middle of a murder investigation?"

"That's the one," I confirmed. "Molly was with me in San Francisco, and we happened to run into him. He took off running as soon as he saw us, but he dropped a big file full of papers. Turns out, those papers are a bunch of evidence that someone on the City Council is indeed pilfering money from the city. There are also some emails to suggest that whoever was stealing the money found out Caitlin was onto them, and asked the person they were stealing money for to take care of Caitlin."

Theo's eyes widened in shock. This time, I didn't think that he was just putting on an act. I knew from the account records that it wasn't likely that his winery was involved in the scandal at all. He was just as surprised by all of this as I had been. Maybe more so, because he probably knew everyone on the City Council. As he furrowed his brow, I imagined that he was running through a list of Councilmember names in his head, wondering which one could have possibly done this.

He shook his head slowly, looking sad. "It's a shame how people will let money drive them to such awful lengths. I guess Mitch will have to run an investigation into the Council to see who's responsible for all of this, and who was colluding with Josie."

"Yeah," I said, and then hung my head sheepishly. "Listen, I'm sorry I accused you of murder. I know we got off on the wrong foot, but perhaps now that the truth on this whole crime is starting to come out, you and I could start over and be friends?"

Theo smiled. "I'd like that very much. And I'm sorry that I gave you such a hard time about being a murderer. For the record, I never truly believed it. It's not like you really had a motive. But you're just so cute when you're flustered and angry. I couldn't stop myself from egging you on."

I blushed, his words making me flustered, which made me realize he must think I was cute at that moment, which flustered me even more.

"It's all right," I stammered out. I couldn't think of what else to say, and Molly's teasing finger poking into my side didn't help. I didn't dare look into her eyes right now: I had a feeling she'd be raising an eyebrow at me or winking in a knowing way to tell me how amused she was that I too had fallen under the spell of Mr. Charming himself, Theo Russo. To avoid looking at Theo or Molly, I glanced over at Scott, thinking that looking at him right now would be a pretty safe bet.

To my surprise, Scott looked angry. He was frowning at Theo, and a moment later he moved protectively to put his arm around me. The warmth of that arm felt good, and I suddenly realized that I had two guys in Sunshine Springs trying to flirt with me at the same time. I hadn't thought the little bit of chemistry between Scott and me had been that serious, but if the way he was acting right now was any indication, it had been.

Before anything could escalate between Scott and Theo, however, Mitch appeared back in the pie shop. He had several bloody scratches on his face and hands from rolling in the glass on the floor when he attacked Josie. Theo had a few scratches too, but Mitch's were worse. It looked like he had actually taken the brunt of

97

everything. He didn't seem bothered by his wounds though. In fact, he seemed quite energized at the moment. I couldn't help but smile as he strode toward us, cracking his knuckles along the way.

Perhaps I'd judged Mitch too quickly as well. Yes, he acted like a macho jerk. But he had just helped to save my life. Maybe he wasn't such a bad man, or such a bad cop. And he'd been right to defend Theo. There wasn't any evidence against Theo after all, and Mitch had known Theo well enough all along to know that Theo was innocent. In any case, now that I was no longer the prime suspect in a murder, I found it a little easier to smile at the Sunshine Springs Sheriff.

"Are you all alright?" Mitch asked as he approached. He shook his head as he glanced over his shoulder. "I can't believe what Josie just did. I have to be honest: I really thought she was the least likely of all the suspects to be the killer. But I guess my instincts are going soft. We don't have any hard evidence to tie her to the poisoning yet, of course. But I think it stands to reason that if she was willing to shoot down the three of you, then she just might have been willing to poison her sister."

"Yeah, about that," Scott said with an awkward cough. "We might have a bit of evidence that Josie was the poisoner, after all."

Mitch raised an eyebrow at Scott. "Oh?"

Scott nodded, looking a bit sheepish. "I suppose I should've told you sooner, but better late than never. There's a guy down in forensics testing some pills that came from Josie's purse. We think they might have been the poison."

Mitch's eyes darkened a little. "Okay. Well, I won't be too hard on you at the moment, considering you almost got your head shot off. But you know that if there were potential poisons in Josie's possession, proper evidence procedures should have been followed or that evidence might not be admissible in court."

Scott looked chastised, and I felt badly for him.

"It was my fault," I said. "I thought you were out to get me, and I thought it was better if I took things into my own hands. But I would assume that if there was poison in Josie's purse, which is where this potential poison came from, she must have more at home or at her hotel room. I bet if you got a search warrant you'd find something more."

Mitch shook his head at me in exasperation. "I told you not to play detective. But you're just like your grandma, aren't you? You do what you want to do, and don't listen to anyone else."

I shrugged at him. He was smiling as he said these words, so I figured I was mostly forgiven. He must've still been happy from the adrenaline rush of tackling Josie. Or maybe he just wasn't that bad of a guy after all. In any case, it felt good not to be hiding things anymore.

Mitch rubbed his forehead, and then looked down at his watch. "It sounds like all of you have quite a bit to tell me. I'd like to take statements, but I don't think it has to be tonight. I'll let you all go home and get some rest if you promise me you'll come by the station in the morning and have a chat with us. We'll be too busy tonight grilling Josie to pay much attention to you three, anyway."

Scott, Molly and I all nodded eagerly. I don't think any of us were too keen on doing anything other than going home and collapsing into bed at the moment. I would have loved to clean up the pie shop first, since shattered glass had been strewn everywhere. But I figured that would have to wait until morning. Mitch already had officers securing it as a crime scene, taking photographs and making notes on little pocket notepads. I sighed as I watched them. Would my pie shop ever go more than a few days without being the scene of a crime? At least, if I was lucky, tonight's events would bring a fresh wave of gossip-seeking customers my way.

Mitch gave each of us his business card, as though we didn't already know who he was or what the police station's phone number was. But I humored him, thanking him for the card. It probably made him feel important to pass them out, and if he wanted to feel important, I wouldn't begrudge him that. Not after what he'd done tonight. Not only had he saved my life, but he'd also promised to post a guard outside my pie shop until I got the door fixed. He didn't have to do that, and I was grateful for his kindness.

As Mitch walked away, Scott finally dropped his arm from my shoulders. I had to admit that I regretted the loss of his warmth. But I knew we all had to get home. I'm sure Scott had an early morning tomorrow with deliveries to make, and besides, this wasn't the best time to explore any feelings I might have for him. I was exhausted, and a mess. My pie shop was also a mess. Besides, I had quite an audience: Molly, who was quickly becoming my best friend and was watching me with eagle eyes; and then Theo, who was also watching closely, but for different reasons. I didn't have the energy to think about making a choice between Theo and Scott right now, nor about whether I was reading both men correctly in assuming they were both interested in me. For heaven's sake, my divorce had only been finalized this morning. I needed to take a few deep breaths, and take some time to recover from the divorce before moving on to any sort of new relationship.

Beside me, Sprinkles whined and nudged my hand with his muzzle, as if to remind me that I still had him, no matter what else was going on. I looked down at him and smiled, giving him a vigorous rub behind the ears.

"You were a good boy tonight. I'm so glad you listened to me. I don't know what I would've done if I'd lost you."

Molly and Scott had walked away to gather up their things, but Theo was still standing there. "Seriously? Did Josie threaten your dog, too?"

I nodded. "Yeah, he was threatening to attack her, so she almost shot him."

Theo shook his head. "That's just wrong. Who kills a dog?"

I laughed. "Well, I agree with you that it's just wrong to kill a dog. But are you really that surprised? If she was willing to kill three humans, then it shouldn't be that surprising that she was willing to kill a dog."

"I suppose you're right. But I just think that anyone who would harm an animal has no soul." Theo crossed his arms and shook his head in disgust. I let myself admire his good looks for a moment. Had he really been flirting with me? Was it possible that this wealthy, handsome bachelor was into me?

I forced myself to push the thoughts away. All of us were high on adrenaline tonight, and I shouldn't read too much into things. I should just be happy that one of Sunshine Springs' most prominent residents seemed to be on good terms with me now. Perhaps my status as an outsider was finally expiring, and I was becoming a local. I didn't want to push my luck on anything beyond that at the moment.

"Well," I said awkwardly. "Thanks again for everything. You know, saving my life and all." I gave a nervous little laugh. "I should get going now, but I'll see you around?"

Theo nodded. "Are you opening the pie shop tomorrow?"

I frowned as I looked around. "I don't think so. I'm not sure when I'll be allowed to clean all this up, but it's already late. I also don't have a front door anymore, and I have a feeling I'm not going to be up for baking a bunch of pies in the morning after almost being shot to death tonight. I think I'll close the shop for one more day."

"Good call. In that case, since you'll be free tomorrow after giving your statement at the police station, why don't you come down to the winery for a private tour?"

I felt a little thrill of excitement. "Really? I'd love that."

"Really," Theo said with a smile. I'd be willing to bet that you could use a day off to just do something relaxing."

"Then you'd bet right," I said with a grin.

I was excited at the prospect of a private tour of Theo's winery. But the truth was, I wasn't sure I could relax in the presence of a man like him. I had a feeling my heart would be racing during the whole tour tomorrow.

Besides that, I wasn't sure I would truly relax until Caitlin's murder case was completely closed. Sure, Josie was in custody now. But we still didn't know the full story. Had she acted alone? Todd was still out there, and it wouldn't be hard for him to find me.

I reached down to rub Sprinkles behind the ears again, thankful that I had him constantly standing guard beside me.

I would definitely be double checking the locks on my doors tonight.

Chapter Sixteen

The next day, after giving my statement at the police station, I headed down to the Sunshine Springs Winery with Sprinkles in the passenger seat beside me. As I parked in the gravel parking lot and the dust settled, I saw that Theo was already waiting for me. In the late morning sunlight, he looked even more handsome than usual. He wore dark wash jeans and a crisp button-down shirt—the perfect blend of casual and professional. I smiled and gave him a small wave before I killed my car's engine and grabbed my purse. What was I getting myself into? I'm sure Molly would not be able to give me enough eye rolls to express her feelings if she knew the thoughts running through my head about Theo. Hopefully, she wouldn't realize for a while yet that I had indeed succumbed to the charms of Theo Russo, just like many a woman before me.

I took a deep breath, and told myself that I was different. I'd been married and divorced, so I knew better than to trust my heart too quickly to a man. I wouldn't let Theo sweep me off my feet as easily as he had any of the other girls. If he was interested in me, he was going to have to work for my heart.

"Hey," Theo said as I strode toward him. He reached down to pet Sprinkles, which made me wonder where his dogs were.

"Don't you have dogs, too? Why don't you bring them out for the tour?"

Theo looked confused for a moment, then laughed. "I don't have dogs. You probably think I do because of the barking you heard the night you and Molly came to accuse me of murder."

I frowned. "Well, yes. Generally hearing dogs barking inside of someone's house means they have dogs."

"Generally, yes. But in my case, the barking is part of my alarm system. It's just a recording that makes people think there's a big, ferocious dog waiting for them if they break in."

I stared at him for a moment. "Are you serious?"

"Yes."

"Why don't you just get real dogs?"

Theo was quiet for a moment. "I had a real dog. He died a year ago, and I haven't been ready to get a new one yet. It would feel too much like replacing him."

"Oh. I'm really sorry. And I'm sorry I brought it up."

I was sorry that I'd brought up what was a sad subject for Theo, but knowing how much he'd cared for his dog only made me like him more.

Theo smiled. "Don't worry about it. I miss him, but he had a good, long life. One of these days, I'll be ready for a new dog. In the meantime, I'll enjoy spoiling my friends' pets. Like this guy right here."

He gave Sprinkles a vigorous rub behind the ear, and my heart warmed even more. Theo was turning out to be a decent guy. I felt my heart skip a beat as he gestured toward the winery with a grand sweep of his hand.

"Ready for your private tour?"

"Ready, indeed. I've never been given a private tour of a winery."

"You're in for a treat. Come on, I'll show you the barrel cellar first."

Over the next hour and a half, Theo led Sprinkles and me through his winery, proudly pointing out the features of his winemaking process that he thought made his wine unique. When we'd looked at everything except the tasting room and the grapevines themselves, Theo asked if I was hungry.

"A little bit," I said. "I didn't eat much for breakfast, so I should probably eat something. I haven't had much of an appetite since last night. Something about almost losing my life seems to have put a damper on my desire for food."

Theo's face sobered, and his eyes clouded over. "I'm sorry. I still can't believe Josie came in there like that. She must have really lost her mind."

I shrugged, not wanting to spoil the magic of this day with thoughts of the horror of last night. "It's not your fault. Let's try to forget about it for now."

"Good idea. But if you *are* hungry, we can go into the tasting room and have some lunch. I usually don't offer a full meal in there, but one of my employees can whip us up a generous plate of the crackers, olives and cheese that we normally serve as side bites for our wine tastings. How does that sound?"

"That sounds perfect. A light lunch in the tasting room is just what I need. I'm assuming there will also be wine available?" I grinned at him.

Theo grinned back. "Of course. You can have as many glasses of whichever wine you want. On the house, even. It's included in the private tour. And I'll find someone to entertain Sprinkles while we're inside." He waved over one of his vineyard employees to take Sprinkles, and then led me into the tasting room.

I'd already seen this room before, of course. But I did enjoy listening to him as he pointed out the features of it that were special to him. When one of his employees called him over to let him know the food was ready, we took our seats at one end of the large bar.

The tasting room was fairly empty today. Theo told me that things would get much busier later in the day. He explained that it was always like that as the weekend approached. The afternoons got crazy busy as people finished up work and headed in from the city in droves. But since things were quiet right now, it was only a few moments before one of the tasting room employees came over to ask me what I would like to drink.

"I'll have a glass of the special 2016 reserve pinot," I said proudly.

Theo laughed when I gave my order. "You must have been here when Violet was here. She tells anyone who will listen that that's the best vintage my winery has, although personally I think the 2015 is better."

"Oh," I said uncertainly. "Then perhaps I should try the 2015?"

"Tell you what. I'll get a glass of the 2015, and you get the 2016. Then you can try both and compare. If you like the 2015 more, you can take my glass. But if, like Violet, you still think the 2016 is better, then I'm not going to argue with you about it. I do believe that subjective taste plays a role in the enjoyment of wine."

I smiled. "Alright," I said, turning to the employee. "Then a glass of the special 2016 reserve it is!"

The employee gave me a funny look, and I decided I must sound a little crazy practically yelling out my wine order. But he recovered quickly, nodded, and went to get my wine for me.

When the glasses of wine came, I had to admit that I honestly couldn't tell much difference between the 2016 and 2015. I let Theo keep the 2015, since he thought it tasted better. It didn't make much difference to me.

As we ate and drank, Theo told me about his father, and how hard he had worked to build up this winery. I told him that Violet had said his father was the best businessman and winemaker in the area, and he smiled.

"She's right. And you're probably leaving out the part where she says that I'll never measure up to him."

I shifted uncomfortably in my seat. "Well, she did sort of say that, but…"

Theo laughed as he took the last swig of what was now his third glass of wine. I finished off my glass too, although I was only on my second. I definitely felt a bit tipsy, probably more due to the excitement of spending so much time with Theo than with the alcohol content of the wine. But I was just going to blame the wine for now. I wasn't quite ready to face my feelings for Theo, or to explore what those feelings might mean.

"It's okay," Theo said with a dismissive wave of his hand. "Violet can sometimes be a little harsh in her judgment of me, but at the end of the day I know she does admire me and my winery. She's one of my best customers. She's always here, and she knows each vintage of my wine by taste. She's also good friends with all of my employees. She's a little strange sometimes, and her anxiety sometimes makes my other patrons uncomfortable. But they can just deal with that. She's a good friend, and she's welcome here anytime she wants to be here. Besides, she's right about me, you know. I do my best, but I'll never measure up to my father."

"Don't say that," I said. "You're fairly young still. You have plenty of time to catch up with your father."

"Well, there's a lot of catching up to do. But anyway, if I become even half the businessman he was, I'll still consider that a wild success." Theo glanced at my empty wine glass. "Would you like another, or are you ready to go see the grapevines?"

"Let's go see the grapevines. Seeing grapevines in sunshine is my favorite part of visiting a winery. Besides, I better slow down on the wine or I'm not going to be able to walk straight through those grapevines."

Theo laughed. "Then grapevines it is."

We made our way out into the grapevines, and Sprinkles happily rejoined us. But the early afternoon sun was stronger than I'd anticipated, and in just a few minutes I was sweating profusely. Theo glanced over at me with concern.

"I forget that not everyone is as used to this sun as I am. Why don't we go up to my house for a bit? There's some shade in the backyard next to a big fountain. It's very peaceful there, and we can relax a bit while you cool down."

I wanted to protest and insist that I was fine, but my discomfort was stronger than my pride. Relieved, I nodded my head and followed Theo to his villa's giant backyard. He picked us each a fresh orange from a tree near the fountain, and we sat below that orange tree's shade as we munched our oranges. Sprinkles settled happily on the grass beside me, his tail thumping out a slow, lazy rhythm. As the sweet juiciness of the orange hit my tongue and revived me, Theo looked off into the distance and started talking about his father again.

"I owe him so much, you know? He left me quite a legacy, and I've done my best to honor that legacy. I've made mistakes, but I'm doing my best." Theo looked over at me, and his eyes had turned uncomfortably serious as he spoke. "I've started to think that perhaps it's time for me to settle down and share that legacy with someone else. But it can't be just anyone else. I need a woman with spunk. A woman not afraid to stand up to me."

I froze with a bite of orange in my mouth. Was he talking about me? I had stood up to him, even if standing up to him had meant falsely accusing him of murder. That had been one of my more ridiculous moments. Still, it had taken a certain amount of guts to just march up to his house in the middle of the night and demand that he confess. I swallowed my bite of orange, and felt my heart beginning to pound as he leaned in toward me, licking his lips.

He's going to kiss me, I thought in surprise. Perhaps even more surprisingly, I wanted that kiss. I started to close my eyes, pushing away all the nagging little voices in my head that told me I was moving on too soon from my divorce, and that I should give myself time to heal. I wanted to enjoy this moment without worrying about all the rules I was supposed to be following. I licked my own lips, and waited for the sparks that I knew were sure to fly the moment his lips connected with mine.

"Theo Russo!"

I jumped at the sudden interruption. The moment broken, my eyes flew wide open, and I turned to see where the voice was coming from. Theo cursed under his breath, but he quickly smoothed away the annoyance on his face and stood to his feet, looking ever like the cool, collected businessman that he was.

"Theo Russo!" The voice yelled again. I turned around, and saw to my surprise that Mitch was walking down the pathway toward us. His face looked drawn and pale, and he had two officers following him.

"Mitch?" Theo asked. "What's wrong?"

Instead of answering Theo directly, Mitch nodded wearily to his officers, who stepped forward and began to pull Theo's hands behind his back.

"Theo Russo, you're under arrest for the murder of Caitlin Dixon. You have the right to remain silent. Anything you say can and will be used against you in a court of law..."

The color drained from Theo's face. "Mitch, what in the world are you doing? I didn't kill anyone! You know that! Don't tell me that crazy Josie girl is somehow trying to pin this on me now. And don't tell me you actually believe her!"

Mitch only shook his head sadly, his voice breaking as he continued on. "You have the right to an attorney..."

I watched in a daze, unsure of what to say or do as the officers started to lead Theo away.

"Mitch," I said, my voice breaking as well. "What's going on here?"

Mitch looked at me with anguish in his eyes. "I'm really sorry. You were right. He had me fooled. He had all of us fooled."

And with that, Mitch hurriedly turned to follow the officers down the path, trying to hide the tears spilling down his normally macho face.

Chapter Seventeen

Shaken, I made my way slowly back to the parking lot and climbed into my car along with Sprinkles. The afternoon crowds for the tasting room were just starting to pick up, and small groups of people stood gawking at the group of police officers as they lead Theo away. The police cruisers left the winery with their lights flashing and sirens blaring, and I wondered if any of those people knew that the man they were watching be arrested was the owner of the winery.

A few of them pulled out their cell phones and snapped pictures, and I wanted to jump out of my car, shake them, and tell them that the destruction of a man's life was not something they should be using to get themselves more likes and comments on their social media pages. But, of course, I didn't get out of my car. I sat there and watched as the crowds pointed and discussed what they'd seen. The inside of the vehicle quickly felt like a furnace, so I turned the engine on to run the air conditioner. I wasn't about to roll down my windows and give anyone a chance to come talk to me.

Eventually, the crowds returned to the tasting room. The excitement was over, and all they really wanted to do was sit around and act like they actually knew which flavor notes each of the Sunshine Springs wines contained.

I sat there for a few more minutes, unsure of what to do. Finally, I realized that I was wasting gas by idling in the parking lot, and I decided to at least start driving toward home. I tried to hold back a choked sob, but it was no use. As I looked at the winery in my rearview mirror, I wondered how I had been so right about Theo, and then so wrong, and then so right again. Or was it the other way around?

All I knew was that I felt confused. I had just convinced myself that he was innocent, and that perhaps there was something between us. I had been about to kiss him, for goodness' sake! I had been about to kiss a murderer.

Alleged murderer, I told myself. I had no idea why he had suddenly become a suspect again. Especially when Mitch hadn't even considered him a suspect in the first place. I had to know what was going on, but I had a feeling that Mitch wasn't going to be in the mood to discuss things with me right now. Unsure of what else to do, I decided to call Scott. I felt a bit guilty as I pulled out my cell phone and hit the call button on Scott's number.

I'd had some sort of feelings for Scott. That much was for sure. And he'd had some sort of feelings for me. But I'd been ready to toss all of that aside for the wealthy, handsome winery owner. And now that that handsome winery owner was under arrest for murder, I needed Scott again, so I was calling him. I'm sure he would understand. He'd told me to call him any time, right? Besides, he didn't know that I'd been on what had practically amounted to a date with Theo. I just wouldn't mention that detail to him, and would hope he didn't find out.

He answered on the first ring. "Izzy?"

"Yeah, it's me. Listen, I was wondering if you've had any deliveries down at the police station today."

"No, I haven't. Although I was there right when they opened this morning to give a quick statement. Why? You wondering what the news is on Josie?"

"Well, not exactly…" I could feel my voice starting to break and betray me. I had to stop and take a deep breath.

"Izzy? Are you all right?"

The concern I could hear in his voice undid me, and the tears started to flow no matter how hard I tried to stop them. "No, I'm not all right. I mean, I'm not in any physical danger. Don't worry about that." I figured that might be where his mind went first, considering the events of last night. "But I was paying a visit to the Sunshine Springs winery just now. You know, trying to get some wine and relax."

I laughed nervously, but trying to make a joke out of the whole situation in a moment like this only made me sound more desperate.

"And? What happened? Are you still at the winery? Are you all right?" I could tell Scott was starting to work himself into a worried frenzy over me. I had to just spit out what had happened or he was going to think that I really was in some kind of mortal danger.

"Mitch just came in here and arrested Theo."

Scott was silent for such a long moment that I thought I might have lost the connection.

"Scott?"

He sighed heavily into the phone. "Yeah, I'm here. Mitch arrested *Theo*? For what? I thought the accounting records for the winery were squeaky clean? Do you think they found something else when they started running a search of the city's email servers?"

"No. Or, well, I don't know. Maybe. But Mitch arrested him for murder. Caitlin's murder. I don't know why. I thought they were pretty clear that Josie had done it. But some new evidence must have come to light, because Mitch wouldn't have arrested one of his best friends unless he was sure that Theo had done something. I was hoping that maybe you'd heard something that would explain what had happened."

"No, sorry. I haven't heard anything. All of the gossip on my route today has been incredibly boring. It's all just stuff about the attack by Josie last night, which obviously I already know about. And it's getting annoying having everyone ask me about it a hundred times in a row."

"Yeah," I laughed weakly. "That's how I felt trying to answer everyone's questions at the pie shop the day after Caitlin died."

There was another long pause, and then Scott sighed into the phone. I could almost picture the look of frustration on his face, and I imagined him running his fingers through his hair in that way he did when he wasn't sure what to do next.

"Tell you what," he finally said. "I'll try to make some calls and talk to a few people to see what I can find out. I'll call you back just as soon as I know something. Where are you now?"

"I'm driving. I'm going to…Well, actually, I'm not sure where I'm going. I was going to go home, but I don't think I can stand being there right now, just pacing around and waiting to hear something. I think I'll go to the Drunken Pie and start cleaning up the shattered glass. I'm assuming the police have gotten all the evidence they need from the crime scene by now."

"Alright, but make sure you stay around a lot of people. I don't want anything to happen to you. Apparently you can't trust anyone in this town."

"I guess not," I said in a small voice. "But I trust you. And I trust Molly. I don't think I'm wrong for that."

"No," Scott said slowly. "You're not wrong for that. I swear to you I'm trustworthy, and I know Molly is too. Don't worry, Izzy. We'll figure this all out. I'll call you as soon as I can, or, if I can manage it, I'll swing by the Drunken Pie. You sure you're alright until then?"

"I'm sure. Thanks a lot, Scott. I really appreciate it."

After I hung up the call with Scott, I headed to the pie shop. I winced as I parked out front. In the sunlight, the jagged edges of broken glass and the bright yellow crime scene tape looked especially harsh. The guard Mitch had promised me stood in front of the pie shop, scrolling on his cell phone. He looked slightly guilty when he looked up and saw me, and he tried to stand a bit more at attention to look like he'd actually been working. I gave him a dismissive little wave of my hand.

"No need to act like you weren't on your phone," I said reassuringly. "I don't mind. I'm sure this job has been mind-numbingly boring. Thanks for watching out for my shop. You can go ahead and go now. I'll be here cleaning things up for the next few hours, and besides, I'm supposed to have a new door delivered anytime now."

The police officer, looking relieved, nodded and thanked me before disappearing down the street.

I stepped into the shop and surveyed the damage. It actually wasn't that bad. There was glass everywhere, and of course the front door was a complete loss. But a local handyman in town had promised me he'd swing by this afternoon and fix it. He'd even said that I didn't need to actually be there for him to do the job, which had been nice when I thought I'd be spending the whole day at Theo's winery. Now, it didn't matter so much. I had nowhere to be but here.

Sprinkles whined as he surveyed the glass, and I turned around to look at him. "Yeah, you don't want to walk across that. You'll probably cut your paws. Here, I'll carry you across to where there's no glass."

I reached down and awkwardly lifted Sprinkles in my arms, just like I used to do when he was a puppy. But he weighed about sixty pounds more now than he had as a puppy, and I worried I was going to strain my back. Still, I did my best to hold him and carefully hobble over the broken glass in the front area of my pie shop. When I finally reached an area that seemed completely free of glass, I set Sprinkles down, then groaned with pain as I stood up.

"You gotta lay off the pie slices, Sprinkles," I said as I rubbed my back.

In response, Sprinkles growled. I rolled my eyes at him.

"Oh, come on. Don't take it personally. I will fully admit that I probably need to lay off of the pie slices, too."

But Sprinkles still didn't seem amused. Instead, his growl deepened, and he bared his teeth. I felt the hair on the back of my neck starting to stand up, and a slow chill spread down my spine. I turned around to look in the direction Sprinkles was looking, and then let out a little shriek.

Todd was standing in between the jagged shards of glass in my broken doorway, and he did not look happy.

Chapter Eighteen

I found myself automatically looking in the direction of Todd's hand, thinking that I was about to see a gun. But Todd's hands were clenched into fists, and I didn't see any weapon of any sort. He could probably do quite a bit of damage with his fists, but I'd take fists over a gun any day.

"What are you doing here?" I asked as soon as I was able to regain my composure a bit.

"I think you know." Todd started walking toward me, that awful, glass-crunching sound echoing across the room with every new step he took. "I want my folder back."

For a moment, I considered playing dumb. But then I thought better of it. I didn't have the folder anymore. If it was the folder he wanted, then maybe he would leave me alone if he realized it wasn't here.

"That folder of evidence is down at the police station where it belongs." I put my hands on my hips indignantly, as though anyone who would keep evidence from the police was a lowlife not worth my time. Of course, I myself hadn't exactly been forthcoming with the police, but Todd didn't need to know that.

The color drained from Todd's face. "Are you serious? Are you an idiot? You turned all of that over to the Sunshine Springs Police Department? That sheriff they have over there couldn't see the truth if it slapped him in the face."

A day or so ago, I might have agreed with Todd. But I was beginning to change my mind about Mitch. He might still be a bit of a big oaf, and I was pretty sure his knuckle-cracking habit would never stop getting on my nerves. But he wasn't all that bad. His methods could be a little bit annoying, but he had a good heart. I had to admit he was doing a better job with the whole murder investigation than I'd originally given him credit for.

I realized with a start that I was defending Mitch in my head. Mitch, whom I'd been sure I would never get along with. Was it possible that I was becoming a true Sunshine Springs local? Despite everything that was going on, the thought made me smile. Todd saw that smile, and didn't take too kindly to it.

"Is this funny to you?" he roared. "I'm under investigation for a murder I didn't commit, and so is Josie. Josie's sister is dead, and while I was never a big fan of Caitlin, I certainly didn't want her dead. I know Josie is completely torn up about it. It ruined our relationship. And now all the notes and evidence Caitlin had that might help me prove who the real killer is have been turned over to the bumbling Sunshine Springs police officers, all thanks to you!"

I hesitated, realizing that Todd must not know that Josie had been arrested. I wasn't sure how much to tell him. I still saw him as the enemy, and my instinct was to not give the enemy any information at all. But if Josie was the murderer, then Todd was probably innocent. And if Theo was the murderer, then Todd was almost definitely innocent. It was looking like odds were good that Todd wasn't the one who killed Caitlin. And if he was innocent, then my heart went out to him. I knew exactly how maddening it was to be falsely accused of murder. I decided to at least catch him up on what was going on here in Sunshine Springs.

"Todd, Josie is being held at the police station. She came in here last night with a gun and threatened to kill me and two of my friends."

"*What?*" Any color that had remained in Todd's face now completely drained away.

"I'm sorry. I guess I didn't realize you didn't know. She came in here demanding that we give the papers back. We didn't argue with her. We weren't really in a position to, since she had a gun and we didn't. But before she could make off with all the papers, the police arrived. They took her into custody, along with all of those papers."

Todd eyed me suspiciously. "You can't be serious. Josie with a gun? I don't think she even knows how to use a gun!"

I gave a dry little laugh. "Well, I think you're right about that. Which is probably a good thing for me and my dog here. If she'd known how to actually aim and use that thing, we'd probably both be dead right now."

Todd sank into one of my café chairs. All the fight seemed to have gone out of him. "I don't believe it," he murmured. He didn't seem to really be talking to me. He was staring off into space, and I got the feeling that he was desperately trying to fight away tears. It was a few moments before he managed to compose himself and look back at me.

"Does this mean that Josie is actually the one who killed Caitlin?" His voice trembled as he spoke, and I felt sort of sorry for him. This whole situation was quite a bit more personal for him than it was for me.

"Well, it certainly seems that way after last night. But now I'm not so sure. I was down at the Sunshine Springs Winery about an hour ago, and while I was there the police came and arrested Theo. So it's looking like maybe your original theory was correct, and that Theo was stealing money from the city. I've said all along that he had the strongest motive of anyone to kill Caitlin. But right now I don't know any more details other than that Theo was arrested for the murder. I don't know if that means Josie's name has been cleared or not."

Todd rubbed his forehead. "God, I hope her name has been cleared. I suppose she'll still be in trouble for trying to shoot you all. But since she didn't actually shoot you, hopefully she'll be in less trouble than she'd be in for murdering someone. I've been trying to get a hold of her all day today and she hasn't answered. Now I understand why. Yesterday, when I realized my papers were missing, I thought maybe you all had taken them somehow. I called Josie and asked her to check into it. I never imagined that she would go crazy like that, or I never would have called her."

"She is under a lot of stress right now," I said gently. "People do some crazy things under stress."

"I suppose you're right. I myself have been a little crazy the last few days. I'm not normally the kind of person who would run away from the law, especially when I know I'm innocent. But I was starting to feel suffocated in this town. That's why I tried to escape to San Francisco, but I guess my escape didn't work out so well. You followed me there and then stole my evidence." Todd slumped in his chair.

"I didn't exactly follow you there. I was in San Francisco for something else, and just happened to see you. But I do understand what you mean. I would be lying if I said I hadn't thought of making a run for it myself."

Todd nodded, but he looked dejected. "I wish I hadn't lost all those documents to you and then the police. Some of them, like the photographs, I have the original files for and can easily reprint. But others, like the emails and account records, I wouldn't know how to replace. Caitlin had somehow gotten them from an anonymous source."

"Well, if it makes you feel any better, I do think that Mitch has turned out to be trustworthy. I know, I know," I said, raising my hands defensively as Todd gave me a look that said he thought I was crazy. "He does come across like a bit of a buffoon. But he has been there in moments when he was truly needed. And the fact that he actually arrested Theo makes me trust him. Theo was one of his best friends, but he still arrested him when he found hard evidence against him. I just have no idea what that evidence was."

Todd still looked doubtful. But before he could answer me, the sound of more crunching glass at the Drunken Pie's front door drew my attention. I looked up, expecting to see the repair man who would fix the door. Instead, Scott stood there. My heart leapt at the sight of him. It was pretty clear at this point that Todd wasn't going to hurt me, but it was still nice to have a friend nearby—just in case.

Scott himself didn't look happy. He was scowling in Todd's direction, and looked like he was about to rush at the man and connect a fist with his face.

"What are you doing here?" Scott demanded of Todd.

I opened my mouth to tell Scott to calm down, but Todd beat me to it. He raised his arms in a gesture of surrender as he spoke.

"Hey, man, don't worry. I'm not going to cause any trouble, and I don't have a gun on me like Josie." He gave a small laugh, but his attempt at a joke fell flat. "I was just here to try to get my evidence back, but I guess it's already down at the police station."

"Todd came to get the papers, not knowing that Josie had already been here last night," I told Scott. "I've just explained to him about Josie, and about Theo. He's quite shaken up. I don't think we need to really shake him up any more."

Scott still looked at Todd warily, but he nodded at me.

"Well, maybe it's good that he's here, then. I have some information he might be interested to hear. I can tell you both at the same time. The test reports came back from the medication we found in Josie's purse."

I stood up straighter, and beside me, Sprinkles' ears perked up as though he understood what was going on.

"And?" I asked. Across the room, Todd was sitting up straighter as well, eager to hear the report.

Scott was shaking his head. "It wasn't poisonous. The pills were simple ibuprofen pills that she was carrying in an unmarked bottle. Mitch has still been working on getting a search warrant for her hotel room, especially since Violet swears she saw Josie put something in Caitlin's glass down at the winery. But I don't think at this point that Mitch is expecting to find much. Apparently, after reviewing the documents Mitch took last night, everyone down at the police station has agreed that the case against Theo is pretty strong."

"Ha! I knew it!" Todd said. "He's the only one whose motive made sense."

I didn't share in Todd's jubilee over the fact that Theo was likely guilty. Instead, I felt sick to my stomach. Theo had really had me convinced earlier today that he was a good guy. Honestly, he seemed exactly as Violet had described him: a hard-working man who was just doing his best to live up to his father's legacy.

Scott's face looked a little sick too. Scott and Theo weren't best friends or anything, but Scott had known Theo for a long time. It must have been quite a shock to see the man accused.

"Did you find out what evidence Mitch found?" I asked, even though I wasn't sure whether I wanted to know the answer anymore.

"Yeah, I overheard some gossip down at the Morning Brew Café. Some officers were in there for lunch at the same time that the historical romance monthly book club was meeting. The ladies in the book club overheard them talking, and now the news is spreading through town like wildfire. It sounds like, after analyzing all of the emails, the evidence strongly points to Theo being the one receiving money from a corrupt City Councilmember."

"But I thought the winery's account records didn't show anything suspicious," I said. I was clinging to any last hope that Theo might be innocent. Funny how things changed. A few days ago, I would have been ecstatic to have even the slightest shred of proof against him.

Scott shrugged. "Well, just because the records we have looked correct doesn't mean those records are accurate. Theo was probably extra careful to hide the money away from the winery's ledgers. In any case, I heard that several of the emails discussed what needed to be done to get rid of Caitlin. The one that we found last night was just the beginning. There were more, and they all talked about how the City Councilmember would be willing to pay extra money to have Caitlin poisoned. For several emails, these two mystery correspondents went on about how to give Caitlin poisoned wine. I guess they knew that she was planning to come to the tasting room soon, and they figured that'd be a good time to take her out. The correspondent whom we're assuming was Theo said that he thought he could get one of the employees in the tasting room to make sure Caitlin only got drinks from a certain bottle of wine—a bottle of wine that was poisoned."

My heart tightened in my chest, and I sank into a chair at the same moment that Todd triumphantly stood up from his.

"I knew it! I knew he was guilty!" Todd fist pumped the air like his team had just won the Super Bowl.

I still didn't want to believe it. Not when I'd been so ready to fall head over heels for Theo. Had I really been that blind?

"But are they absolutely sure the correspondent was Theo?" I asked. "Were they able to figure out which email addresses had been blacked out?"

Scott shook his head. "Yes, but that didn't help them much. In fact, it wouldn't have mattered if the copies Caitlin had received hadn't been blacked out, because the addresses themselves don't give anything away. They're some sort of nonsense email addresses, no doubt made up to be used just for the purpose of carrying out this scheme. But from what I heard, the emails leave little doubt that Theo is the one behind all of this. The messages all discuss the winery and its wines in detail, and they even talked about getting the tasting room employees on board with the scheme. If Theo wasn't responsible for that, it would at least had to have been someone higher up at the winery—someone who had a great deal of knowledge about the place. And there honestly aren't too many people like that. Theo doesn't really have any other top level employees. The winery is his baby, and he prefers to do everything that he possibly can himself."

I leaned onto the table in front of me, putting my head in my hands. Sprinkles sidled up beside me and laid a comforting paw on my leg. I reached down to pet him, but I still felt forlorn. I should be ecstatic about this. My name was all but cleared of murder, and with Josie and Todd likely to be cleared as well, I probably wouldn't have to worry about any more angry visits from them either. So why did I still feel so upset?

Scott seemed to sense my despair. "I know it's a lot to take in," he said. "Why don't you sit there and rest for a little bit. I'll make you some coffee."

As he walked around the counter to get the coffee machine going, the phone line for the Drunken Pie Café rang. Scott glanced at it.

"Do you want to get that?" he asked. "I'm sure whoever it is would understand if you weren't answering your phone today."

"No," I said wearily. "I should get it. It might be the repairman for the door. He has my cell number, but I think I forgot my cell phone in my car. Maybe he's trying to reach me this way."

I stood and walked toward the counter. Scott handed the cordless handset to me, and I hit the answer button.

"Drunken Pie Café." I tried to keep my voice as chipper as possible under the circumstances.

"Oh, thank goodness. I've been trying to call your cell phone, but you're not answering it."

"Who is this?" The male voice sounded slightly familiar, but he didn't sound like the repair man.

"Oh, sorry. It's Mitch. Listen, I know it's been a crazy couple of days, but could I bother you to come down the street to the station as soon as possible?"

"I suppose so," I said slowly. "But why? I already gave my statement this morning. Did you need something else from me?"

There was a long, loud sigh on the other end of the line. "Yes, I need something. Well, actually, Theo needs something."

"Okay…" I said slowly.

"Theo is asking to speak to his lawyer, and he's saying that you're his lawyer."

"What? That's ridiculous. I *am* a lawyer, but I'm a contracts lawyer. Not a criminal lawyer. He needs a criminal lawyer. And besides, I'm trying to get out of the lawyer business. That's why I moved here and opened my café."

"I know," Mitch said. "Trust me. I tried to explain all of that to him, but he won't listen. He's saying that he has a right to speak to his lawyer, and that his lawyer is you. To be honest, he's driving me a little bit bananas. Would you mind just coming down to talk to him for a minute? As a favor to me, even? Maybe if he hears it straight from you that you're not a criminal lawyer, then he'll stop being so ridiculous."

It was my turn to sigh. As much as I wanted to help Theo, there was no way I was taking on a criminal case. But I supposed it wouldn't hurt to talk to him. Besides, I was interested in learning more about this sudden turn of events in Caitlin's murder case. Maybe being down at the station and talking to Theo would shed new light on the situation.

"Okay," I said. "If Theo wants to talk to me, then I'll come talk to him. I'll be there in about fifteen minutes."

When I hung up the phone, Scott gave me a curious look. "What was that all about?"

"It was about Theo. He wants to talk to me, so I'm going to go down to the station."

"Talk to you about what?" Scott asked.

"No idea. But I can't help hoping that he might know something that would still prove his innocence." I deliberately avoided looking at Todd as I said this. I'm sure Todd must've thought I was crazy. Here I was on the verge of being acquitted of Caitlin's murder, and I was trying to stir up proof that the alleged murderer was innocent? And yet, something about all of this still didn't sit right with me.

"Do you mind watching the shop until the door repairman gets here?" I asked Scott. "If you don't have more deliveries to do, that is."

"I don't mind at all. I'll keep Sprinkles with me too. All on the condition that I can have as much coffee as I want, and that you'll give me the full scoop on what Theo says when you get back."

I smiled. "Deal."

I continued to ignore Todd as I headed out to the police station to find out just what that scoop might be.

Chapter Nineteen

When I arrived, the police station was in a state of chaos. The excitement over Caitlin's murder case had reached fever pitch here in little old Sunshine Springs. Locals filled the reception area, demanding to know what the case against Theo was. The harried receptionist looked miserable as she tried to explain over and over that she didn't know what was going on, and that besides she couldn't comment on an ongoing investigation. She brightened up considerably when she saw me.

"Miss James," she said as she stood. She must have been happy to have something to do other than field inquiries from nosy townspeople. "Sheriff Mitchell has been waiting for you. Follow me, please."

Turning to the crowd, she waved her hands at them in a shooing motion. "As I've said, I have nothing to tell all of you. And now, if you'll excuse me, I need to get Miss James back to see the sheriff."

"Why?" one of the townspeople asked. "Is she being accused of murder, too?"

I wanted to roll my eyes. I'd already been accused of murder, and he knew that. I could have defended myself in that moment, and told him that I'd been acquitted. But that was exactly what they all wanted, wasn't it? To know where the case stood, and where I stood in the case. They wanted the latest gossip. I took great pleasure in keeping my mouth shut and smiling sweetly at them as I followed the receptionist down the hallway to the back of the station. I will admit to being a bit of a gossip-lover myself. But I don't love it when the gossip is about me. What can I say? I'm only human.

The receptionist led me to Mitch's office. When he saw me, he jumped up from behind his desk.

"Oh, thank God. Theo is in a state, let me tell you. A state!" Mitch cracked his knuckles, and for once the gesture came across as nervous instead of aggressive. His face looked pale, and my heart went out to him. This couldn't be easy for him.

"Here I am," I said, a little too brightly. I found myself wanting to say something to make him feel better, but I wasn't sure what. Sorry your best friend turned out to be a murderer? Don't worry, I'm sure there's been a mistake and we'll get this all figured out?

I had no idea what the truth really was here, and I had no idea how to comfort a man like Mitch.

Thankfully for both of us, Mitch seemed to take comfort in the mere act of starting to walk down the hall toward the jail cells. It was probably an easy role for him to fall into: the sheriff in charge. I had a feeling he was grasping onto that role with everything he had right now.

I wish I had a role to grasp onto. I definitely didn't feel like a lawyer anymore, but I wasn't sure I could call myself a pie shop owner, either. In the week or so that I'd been open for business, I'd already been closed several times for a divorce proceeding, an assault against me, and a poisoning. Not exactly a stellar first week of business, if you asked me.

Mitch motioned to an empty interrogation room on our left.

"Go ahead and sit in there," he said. "I'll get Theo and bring him to you. You can talk to him as long as you want."

I nodded, and waited for what seemed like an eternity in the little room. In reality, it was probably less than three minutes until Theo appeared. Mitch nodded to both of us politely, then closed the door to give us privacy. For a few very long moments, Theo and I just stared at each other. He was still wearing the button-down shirt and jeans he'd been wearing earlier in the day, but his face looked older. I wasn't sure whether it was the harsh lights of the interrogation room, or the strain of being accused of murder, but he looked like he'd aged ten years in the last few hours. The dark circles under his eyes definitely hadn't been there when he'd been about to kiss me under the orange tree.

"Hey," I finally said in a soft voice. "How are you?"

"Miserable. I feel badly for ever thinking it was appropriate to tease you about being falsely accused of murder. You were right. There's nothing funny about this."

I felt a spark of hope in my chest. "So this is a false accusation?"

I desperately wanted to believe that it was. Please, Theo, I pleaded silently. Tell me this is all a mistake. Tell me you have some sort of hard evidence to show that it definitely wasn't you.

He let out his breath in a long, exasperated sound. "It's definitely a false accusation. I suppose I deserve it if you don't believe me, but I swear to you that I didn't kill the girl. I've made a lot of mistakes in my life, but murder isn't one of them. Neither is stealing money from the City Council. I don't mean to sound crass, but I'm an incredibly wealthy man. I have more money than I know what to do with. Why would I need to steal money from Sunshine Springs? I love this city, and its people. This is my home. I'm not trying to cheat anyone here out of money that rightfully belongs to them."

"I believe you, Theo. Or, at least, I want to believe you. But it sounds like the evidence against you is pretty bad. You know Mitch wouldn't have arrested you if it wasn't."

"I know what those emails said. Mitch told me. But I swear to you I didn't write them. I don't know who did. Maybe one of my employees thought I wasn't paying them enough and tried to get something on the side from the city. I have a hard time believing that, because I always prided myself on paying the best wages in the business. But maybe it wasn't enough. In any case, there isn't really any hard evidence on me. They don't have my name on those emails, and there's a reason for that: it's because those emails didn't come from me. I might be the first person you think of when you read about poisoning someone in the tasting room. But there are a lot of other people with access to the wines in there."

"I understand. But why did you call me here? I can tell you that I believe you all I want, but it's not my opinion that matters. It's the opinion of the judge or jury when you stand trial."

"I called you here because I need your help. I need you to find a way to prove my innocence. You're a lawyer. You must know something about how to prove innocence in a murder case."

"Theo, I'm a contracts lawyer. I spent my entire legal career arguing over whether this word or that word would get some faceless corporation more or less money out of a deal. Those skills aren't going to do you any good in a murder case. You need a criminal lawyer."

"No!" Theo insisted, slamming his fist on the table for emphasis. "I need you. I need someone smart who truly believes me. You do believe me, don't you?"

"Of course I believe you," I said. And it was true. I really was starting to believe him. I never wanted to believe he was guilty in the first place. Well, not since deciding that I thought he was a good man, after all. There was that brief time at the beginning where I didn't trust him.

But now? Now I believed he was innocent. I just didn't think I was the one to prove his innocence.

I decided to attempt a little bit of humor. "But I'm not smart. You know that. Remember how I marched up to your house in the middle of the night, thinking I could make you confess? Who does that? Not someone smart, that's for sure."

He wasn't impressed with my attempt at humor.

"You are smart. Stop acting like you aren't. I know that whole middle of the night visit was Molly's idea, anyway. It's totally her style, and she just had you along for the ride. She's a great gal, but a little crazy sometimes. As for you, you have guts. I need you on my side right now. Is it money you want? I won't ask you to work as my lawyer for free. I'll pay you whatever you want. Just tell me you'll help me."

I felt my cheeks flush red. "It's not about money, Theo. You're my friend, and I'll help you any way I can. I just think you need a criminal lawyer."

"No. I need you. Please, Izzy. If you care about me at all—as a friend or as…something more. Please help me. If you don't want to call yourself my lawyer, then don't. Call yourself a detective, or even just a friend who wants to help. But promise me you'll find evidence to get me out of here."

I chewed my lower lip for a moment. What could I say? If I thought he was innocent, and a big part of me did, then what kind of friend would I be if I didn't at least try to help him?

Slowly, I nodded. "Okay. I'll help you. But you have to understand that I can't be your lawyer. I can only be your friend. And as a friend, I promise you I'll do everything I can to get you out of this situation."

Relief flooded Theo's face. "Thank you," he said, his voice breaking. "When I get out of here, I promise you I'll make it up to you. Money, wine, someone to vouch for you in the community… Whatever you need, whatever you want—it's yours."

"I'm not doing this for payment. I'm doing it because it's the right thing to do."

Theo nodded, his eyes looking suspiciously moist. All of these macho men who were suddenly breaking down in tears were making me feel disconcerted. I supposed it was to be expected in situations like this. Having your life turned upside down by a murder accusation was bound to make even the toughest guy a little emotional.

I decided the best thing to do here was to focus on taking action. If Theo felt like I was taking action, then hopefully he would take heart, and at least have something to focus on besides the bad.

"Is there anything you can tell me that might be helpful?" I asked. "Any of your employees at the winery whom you suspect might not be completely upright and honest?"

Theo shook his head slowly. "There's no one in particular, unfortunately. All of my long-term employees I would trust with my life. The guys in the tasting room are seasonal employees. They're interns who come through for the busy summer season or the busy holiday season. But I hardly ever get the same intern twice, so I never really get to know them that well. I would say they're the most likely suspects. But I couldn't point to any particular one of them and say I thought they were the one."

I considered this. "Okay. Well, at least knowing that the tasting room employees are the most likely suspects gives me a place to start. I'll head to the winery and see if I can get any more information on any of them. I'm sure Scott and Molly will be happy to help me as well. No one in Sunshine Springs wants to see one of the locals put away. Especially not an innocent local."

Theo thanked me again, and then I went to call Mitch to let him know we were done. Once Theo had been returned to his cell, I went to Mitch's office to talk to him. Mitch greeted me with a tired but sincere smile.

"So? How did it go? Did he convince you to be his lawyer?"

"No." I flopped into the rickety guest chair in Mitch's office. "But he did convince me that he's innocent, and that I should help find evidence to prove it."

Mitch grimaced. "I don't have to tell you that I hope you're right and that he is innocent. But I do have to tell you that the evidence against him looks pretty bad."

"He told me. But he made a good point: anyone at the winery could have been responsible for those emails. Sure, Theo would have been the most able to carry out a scheme like slipping a bottle of poisoned wine into the mix when Caitlin visited. But it's not impossible that it was someone else."

"I know it's not impossible. It's just unlikely. In fact, it's so unlikely that our local judge has insisted that we not allow Theo to post bail. That's why he's still in here."

"And Josie? Is she still in here?"

Mitch leaned back in his creaky office chair. "Yep. She's still here. She can't get out on bail either, considering that she violated our trust on the first round of bail by attacking you guys. But at least she's pretty much off the hook for the Caitlin murder. We're almost certain she had nothing to do with it. I'm assuming Scott's already told you that the pills you guys took from her weren't poisonous?"

I blushed. Mitch knew all too well that Scott was privy to most of the gossip in town, and that he happily passed that gossip along to me. There was no sense in denying it. "Yes, Scott told me. I'm sorry we troubled you with all of that."

Mitch waved away my apology. "Don't worry about it. That was a line of evidence we were investigating anyway, since Violet insisted she saw Josie put something in Caitlin's drink. But I don't think anything's going to come of that. It was always a bit of a weak case against Josie. After all, you have to be a special brand of awful to kill your own sister. Maybe Caitlin was putting something completely benign in her sister's drink, like ground-up pain medication. Or maybe Violet misunderstood what she saw. Violet's a good lady, but she is a little bit old and nervous. And maybe a little bit crazy."

"Yeah, a little bit crazy is putting it nicely. But I guess once you get to that age you're allowed to be a little bit crazy."

"Like your grandma, huh?" Mitch teased. "She's about as crazy as they come."

I stuck my tongue out at him. "Grams might be crazy, but at least she's not insanely anxious. I don't know if I could live with that kind of anxiety. Violet should go see a shrink or something."

Mitch shrugged. "Yeah, well she's old and set in her ways. Good luck getting her to change. But anyway, all that to say that it looks like Josie is innocent, at least of Caitlin's murder. It will be up to you, Scott and Molly whether we charge her with assault for coming at you with the gun. But until we get all that sorted out, she'll stay here behind bars."

"Honestly, I don't care that much what happens to Josie at this point. Maybe you should talk to Scott and Molly and see how they feel, but it doesn't make much difference to me whether she's charged or not. I don't want her coming after me to attack me again, but since I don't have the records she wants anymore, I'd guess she has very little interest left in me."

"You're probably right. My guess is that if we set Josie free, she's going to get as far away from Sunshine Springs as she can as quickly as she can."

I nodded, and then stood. "Well, I guess I should get started on proving Theo's innocence, although I don't really know where to start. I don't suppose I could take a look at all of those records you have again?"

Mitch shook his head apologetically. "No, sorry. I can't release evidence, especially if you're not actually Theo's lawyer."

For a moment, I had the crazy idea to agree to be Theo's lawyer just so I could look through the evidence. But I pushed that idea away. If it came to the point that he was brought before the court and needed a lawyer, he needed a criminal lawyer. Besides, it sounded like I already had a pretty good idea of what was in the emails.

In fact, it sounded like the whole town had a pretty good idea of what was in the emails. I'm sure if I had more specific questions I could figure out a way to get the information I needed.

"Alright," I said. "I'm gonna get going then."

"Where will you go?" Mitch asked.

I smiled at him. "To Grams' house, I think. Sometimes, when you can't figure out what to do, talking to a crazy old lady who loves you more than anything can do wonders to help you figure it out."

Chapter Twenty

After a quick call to Scott to make sure that he was okay hanging out at the café with Sprinkles for a little bit longer, I headed to Grams' house. When I got there, I saw Violet's giant white Buick sitting out front. I groaned, and seriously considered turning around to come back later. I wasn't sure I was in the mood for Violet's type of crazy right now. But before I could make the decision to drive away, Grams and Violet both appeared on Grams' front porch. Grams saw me, and gave an excited wave.

I was caught. There was no way I was getting away without spending at least a little bit of time here. Groaning to myself, I got out of the car and forced a wide smile onto my face.

"Grams," I greeted her. "And Violet. Nice to see you both."

Grams grinned at me. "You're in luck. I've got a fresh pitcher of sun tea, and I baked a lemon cake this morning. I'm sure the cake isn't as good as your pies, especially not the boozy pies, but it's not too bad if I do say so myself."

I resisted the urge to groan again. If Grams had sun tea and lemon cake, that meant I would have to stay for a while, sipping tea and eating cake while listening to her and Violet prattle on about the minutest details of Sunshine Springs gossip. But I stuffed my feelings down and kept the smile on my face.

"Wonderful! I'd love to sit and have tea and cake with you and Miss Violet."

"Oh, I was actually just leaving," Violet said. "I've been here for a while already, and I have an appointment for a massage down at the spa. Goodness knows I need all the relaxation I can get with all of this hullabaloo lately about Caitlin's murder."

I nodded sympathetically, not mentioning the fact that I didn't think all of the massages in the world could massage away the amount of anxiety Violet kept pinned up inside that shaky body of hers.

"Well, I'm sorry I missed you then," I lied. "But I hope you enjoy the spa."

"I will," Violet assured me. "And I'm glad to see you here spending time with your grandmother instead of going off and playing detective. I suppose you finally learned your lesson after that crazy Josie girl came and attacked you at your café. Better to leave these sorts of things to the professionals."

I decided now was not the best time to mention that I had just agreed to do some detective work for Theo. Violet would be worried that I was going to mess up Theo's case by sticking my nose into it, so I waited until Violet's noisy Buick was halfway down Grams' street before I admitted to Grams why I was really there.

"Theo asked me to be his lawyer."

I expected Grams to laugh out loud at this. To my surprise, she only raised one slightly quizzical eyebrow. "Did he now?"

She motioned for me to follow her to the back porch, where she had a pitcher of sun tea just as she'd promised. Next to the lemon cake, she'd set out enough plates that you'd think she was about to throw a full-on garden party. She also had on what I would consider a fancy party dress—it was frilly and hot pink. She'd accented it with a hot pink fashion hat and lime green necklaces and bracelets. On her feet, she wore bright orange sandals. I glanced over her outfit and the numerous place settings on her patio furniture, and it was my turn to raise an eyebrow.

"Expecting company?"

Grams shrugged. "You never know. It's best to be prepared, especially when you bake a lemon cake. Somehow, every time I bake a lemon cake, folks start magically showing up at my front door. It's like word quickly gets around that there's lemon cake here. And you know everyone in town loves my lemon cake. In fact, you should sell it at your pie shop. I bet it'd be a bestseller, especially if you added alcohol to it. Boozy lemon cake! Can you imagine?"

Grams closed her eyes in rapture, as though nothing in the world could possibly make her as happy as the mere idea of boozy lemon cake.

I couldn't help but chuckle. "I'd be happy to sell lemon cake at my pie shop. But you won't give up the recipe."

"True, true. I can't be too careful guarding that secret. But don't worry. I've bequeathed the recipe to you in my will. So when I croak, then you can serve lemon cake at the Drunken Pie Café in my honor." Grams beamed happily as though she hadn't just referenced her own death.

"Grams! Don't talk like that! I don't even want to think about you not being here anymore."

Grams laughed. "Don't worry, dear. I don't plan on dying for a long time. But it is a fact of life that I'm going to die at some point. When I do, that lemon cake recipe is coming your way. Now, enough with all of that. Tell me what's going on with Theo."

Grams put a generous slice of lemon cake on a plate for me as I began to explain everything to her. I told her the entire story, from the moment I'd run into Todd in San Francisco all the way up to the moment less than an hour ago when I told Theo I would do everything I could to prove his innocence. The only small detail I left out was the fact that Theo and I had almost kissed. But I had a feeling that Grams knew about that, anyway. She always seemed to know when I liked a guy before I even knew myself.

When I'd finished telling her everything, she was silent for several moments. I took a big sip of sun tea, and hoped that she was going to have something helpful to say. But all she said when she finally did speak was, "Humph."

"Humph?" I asked. "That's all you have to say?"

Grams shrugged. "What should I say? It sounds like everything is clear. Theo's innocent, and you've agreed to help prove it. Sounds like a good plan to me."

"I'm not sure it's that simple. I really do think he's innocent, but I have no idea how to go about proving it. I was hoping that you had some sort of ideas on how to help me."

Grams laughed merrily and waved her hand at me. Her lime green beaded bracelets clanked against each other as she did.

"Now, why on earth would I know what to do? I'm just an old lady who likes to sit around eating lemon cake. I don't have the faintest idea how to go about conducting a murder investigation."

"But," I said, somewhat desperately. "You *always* know what to do. And you know this town so well. You're the one who told me everything would work out to prove I was innocent. I have to admit I was quite irritated with you for being so confident of that—"

"I noticed," Grams interrupted in a dry tone.

"I'm sorry for doubting you," I continued. "But now I'm here admitting that I was wrong. I'm admitting that I need your help. You must understand something about how these things work, because you knew everything would work out for me. And I know you think Theo is innocent. You must have reasons for that, too. Tell me what to do, Grams. Where do I even start to look for evidence in this town?"

Grams smiled at me. "Izzy, I knew that everything would work out to prove your innocence because I know you are innocent. And the truth always prevails. Sometimes, you have to help it along a little bit, but the truth does always prevail. I believe Theo is innocent, so the truth will prevail in his case as well. You're a smart girl. Figure out how to help the truth along here. Put your head together with Scott and Molly and figure out a way. I might have joined you in my younger days, but these days I'm too old to be gallivanting around chasing down a murderer. Just follow your heart, and it won't lead you wrong."

"Seriously? Follow your heart? That's the best advice you can give me?"

Grams reached across and affectionately stroked my cheek with her thumb. "Yes. Follow your heart. I believe in you. If anyone can do this, it's you. I would only slow you down, and besides, I need to keep an eye on Violet."

"Violet? How long are you going to let her ride this 'poor old me' act? She didn't even actually kill Caitlin. She just ran into Caitlin's dead body. Why is she still so upset?"

"Isabelle James! Have a little bit of sympathy for the old woman. She already deals with such bad anxiety that she can hardly walk straight. This whole ordeal has really set her off."

"I'm sorry," I said, even though I didn't feel very sorry. "I guess I'm just a little bit salty because she doesn't think I can handle being a detective."

Grams shrugged. "What can I say? She's old and set in her ways. Don't let it get to you. You just concentrate on helping Theo and let the naysayers say what they will. I believe in you. And if your Grams believes in you, shouldn't that be all that matters?"

I sighed and reached over to give Grams a hug. "Yes, you're right. It's all that matters."

Before I had even finished hugging her, the loud, musical sound of her front doorbell drifted out onto the patio through the open back door. Grams looked at me and winked.

"I had a feeling I'd have more company soon. I'm sure Violet let it slip to anyone she met that I baked lemon cake today."

I followed Grams to the front door, and when she opened it, two white-haired ladies stood there, each wearing floral dresses and straw sun hats.

"Rose! Matilda!" Grams greeted them. "How lovely to see you."

"Agnes," said one of the ladies. "We just happened to be in the neighborhood, and I mentioned to Matilda here that it's been a while since we've seen you. We thought we'd stop by and see if you happened to have time for a quick little chat."

"Of course, dears. And you are in luck! I just so happened to bake a lemon cake today. Would you like a slice?"

"Oh, we couldn't possibly impose," one of the ladies said.

"I insist," Grams said. "I was just saying goodbye to my granddaughter. Run along to the back patio. You know the way?"

The ladies nodded.

"Very well," Grams said. "Go ahead and make yourselves comfortable, and I'll be there in just a moment."

As soon as they disappeared onto the patio, Grams turned and winked at me. "See? What'd I tell you? Word gets out fast when I bake a lemon cake."

I laughed. "Well then, I won't keep you any longer. You have lemon cake to serve, and I have a murder to solve."

"Yes, you do. And solve it you will. Just follow your instincts, darling. They won't lead you astray."

I hugged Grams goodbye and got into my car. I wasn't sure that I bought into the idea that instincts alone would be enough to solve this murder. But somehow, knowing that Grams believed in me did help.

I decided to take the one piece of concrete advice she had given me. I would put my head together in a meeting with Scott and Molly. In fact, I thought it might not be a bad idea to include Todd. He wasn't exactly my favorite person, but he was well-acquainted with the case. He might be able to give us information on how things had played out on that fateful day of Caitlin's death.

I pulled out my cell phone to make some calls. It was time for a meeting of the minds at the Drunken Pie Café.

Chapter Twenty-One

By the time Scott, Molly, Todd and I all arrived at the Drunken Pie Café, the sun was setting and twilight had taken over Sunshine Springs. I poured out glasses of wine for everyone, regretting that I didn't have pie to offer as well. But the last few days had been so chaotic that I hadn't baked anything. Sprinkles looked at me forlornly, and I shook my head at him.

"Sorry, boy. I would give you something if I had it. But you know I've been running around the last few days and haven't baked anything. I promise I'll give you some pie tomorrow."

With a long sigh, Sprinkles flopped on the ground by my feet, resigned to his pie-less fate.

I sat down and looked around at the group seated at the table with me. Scott and Molly looked eager, while Todd looked slightly skeptical. I couldn't blame him. I was asking a lot of him by asking him to trust me. Then again, he was asking a lot of me by expecting me to trust him. We were both just going to have to deal with the uncertainties we felt and press forward.

"Does anyone have a suggestion on where we should start?" I began. "As I told you all on the phone, Theo asked me to prove his innocence. He swears to me that he didn't commit the murder, and I'm inclined to believe him. But that leaves us at a complete dead end. If he's innocent, and Josie's innocent as Mitch seems to think now, then who killed Caitlin?"

Molly frowned as she lifted her wine glass to her face. "Look, you know that I'm not one to point fingers at Theo. But things aren't looking good for him. The emails do implicate his winery. Besides, remember that he was meeting with the mayor? We still haven't figured out what that was all about. I hate to say it, but is it possible it *was* him? I mean, I hope it's not. But we have to explore all angles here."

I had almost forgotten about the meeting with the mayor at this point. I'd become so convinced of Theo's innocence before he was arrested that I hadn't thought about it for a while. It certainly hadn't been on my mind when I'd been about to kiss Theo under the orange tree. I blushed at the thought, and looked down at my wine glass in hopes that no one else would notice my cheeks turning pink. I took a deep breath to steady my emotions, and considered whether I thought a meeting with the mayor played into this at all.

"I did think that meeting was strange at the time I saw it," I said. "But now I have to think that it wasn't anything shady. After all, Mitch was part of that meeting, too. If they were meeting about something related to the murder, or to stealing the city's money, then Mitch would have already known Theo was involved. Why would he suddenly arrest him today? And why would he look completely shell shocked while arresting him? It was like he'd never expected this in a million years."

Scott shrugged. "Maybe Theo had been trying to buy Mitch into the scheme to protect himself. Mitch could have refused, and that's how he knew about Theo's guilt."

I shook my head. "That doesn't really make sense either. I'm telling you, Mitch really looked blindsided by Theo's guilt when he made the arrest. If he did know beforehand, and wasn't going to join Theo in some sort of pilfering scheme, then why would he have waited so long to arrest him?"

Scott shrugged again. "You've got me there. This whole thing is so confusing. I'm not really sure how to solve this."

"We should focus on what we do know," Todd said, speaking up for the first time. "Rehashing dead clues is only going to waste time and frustrate us all."

"What do you suggest?" I asked.

"Well," Todd said. "We do know that an employee at the tasting room was involved. Or at least it's very likely. It seems that whoever committed Caitlin's murder had paid off an employee to be involved and to somehow give her poisoned wine. Perhaps we should see if we can figure out which employee seems suspicious, and then work backwards from there."

This seemed like as good a plan as any to me. "Okay. Let's do that then. All of us here have been to the tasting room before. Can anyone remember off the top of their head whether any of the employees seemed especially suspicious?"

We all thought for a few moments, but in the end no one could remember seeing anything that struck them as out of the ordinary.

"Well then," I said. "I guess we'll have to figure out a way to investigate the tasting room employees further." I turned to look at Todd. "Todd, didn't you say that you had a lot more photos of the tasting room from the day Caitlin died?"

"Yeah, I've got hundreds more photos. When I was trying to put together evidence, I only printed out the ones with Caitlin in them. But there are a lot more. The day we visited the winery, I was trying to take photos of every aspect of the tasting room. I figured it would be good to have some photos of what the place looked like if we did publish an article about it."

I nodded. "Okay, good. Why don't we all look through the digital files together? Maybe if we review everything, there will be something in one of those photos that gives us a clue. Maybe an employee in the background doing something that looks suspicious?"

Everyone agreed, and we reviewed photos for the next two hours. We went through three bottles of wine and about a thousand photos, but nothing seemed out of the ordinary. The photos showed scenes that seemed typical for any tasting room in wine country. There were employees passing out wine and smiling at customers. There were some photos of the historical wall, which showed the pictures of the winery's history. I saw the familiar photo that Violet had pointed out to me of her and Theo's father, the elder Mr. Russo.

"Man, they were both lookers back in their day, huh?" I commented as I pointed to the photo of the old photograph.

Molly laughed. "Yeah, from what I hear, old Mr. Russo had as many girls chasing after him in his day as Theo does now. But when Mr. Russo's wife died not long after Theo was born, he never remarried. He was heartbroken over her loss. I've heard that he dated around a little bit, because everyone pressured him to move on. He even dated Violet for a bit. But in the end, no one could ever replace his first wife, and he decided not to try. He poured his whole life into the winery and into Theo."

I shook my head sadly as I looked down at the picture. "He looks like a nice guy. It's too bad he had to go through so much sadness. I bet he would've made a good husband if he had remarried."

"Yeah," Scott said. "But maybe if he had remarried his winery wouldn't have been so successful. He really poured his heart and soul into it. What a legacy he left for Theo."

I chuckled. "Now you sound like Violet. Every time I talk to her, she's ranting about Mr. Russo and the legacy he left behind. I think she still might not be completely over him."

Molly laughed. "I think you're right. It was a little ridiculous that she thought she was going to get him anyway. She was fifteen years older than him. Seems like a bit of a stretch when there were so many younger women chasing after him. But she was tenacious, and she *did* get him to date her for a while. Never could seal the deal though."

"Sometimes she acts like she's still trying to seal it," Scott said with a roll of his eyes. "Look at how many of these photos she's in. She's always down at that tasting room. She spends the majority of her free time there, like she expects Mr. Russo to come back from the dead, waltz in, and see that she's been waiting for him all these years. It's a wonder her liver hasn't failed with all the wine she drinks."

"She does seem to be there more often than not," I agreed. I decided not to rehash the fact that she'd accused Josie of putting something in Caitlin's drink that day. No one seemed to think that shaky old Violet was a reliable witness, but I wondered if she'd seen anything else that day that might be helpful. I didn't think anyone had interviewed her too seriously. The cops were all afraid of setting off her anxiety, so they went way too light on the questions with her.

I wondered if somehow I could get her to talk. Maybe I could lure her to my pie shop and ply her with chocolate pie to get her to spill the beans on anything else she might have seen. If anyone could tell us about the employees, it would be Violet. But I didn't want to mention in front of Todd the idea of talking to her. He was still angry at her for her role in implicating Josie, so I tucked away the idea of talking to Violet. Maybe later I would talk to her on my own, if the four of us here couldn't manage to figure anything out.

We reviewed photos for about fifteen more minutes, but all that remained were pictures of smiling customers, and then outdoor pictures of the grapevines. I finally admitted defeat and sank back into my chair.

"I think we should call it a night. I'm exhausted, and there doesn't seem to be anything here."

"I hate to say that I agree with you," Molly said. "But what are our next steps? Since there's nothing helpful in the photos here, what do we do?"

"What if we all head down to the tasting room together?" Scott asked. "We could spend a couple hours there tomorrow evening, having a tasting and observing the employees. Maybe if we're all there looking around together, something will spark an idea on what might've happened."

We all agreed that it was as good an idea as any, so I cleaned up our wine glasses and we all headed home. But I couldn't keep myself from feeling like a bit of a failure. I had known better than to expect to find a blazingly obvious clue in Todd's photos. Still, I had hoped. How could I not hope? The image of Theo's pleading eyes in that interrogation room had embedded itself deep in my mind.

I had to find a way to help him. Our group's little rendezvous at the tasting room tomorrow couldn't come soon enough.

Chapter Twenty-Two

I would have loved nothing more than to spend the entire next day playing detective. But I'd already had the pie shop closed more days than open since my grand opening, and I figured I should probably make an effort at having a normal day of business.

Besides, Molly and Scott couldn't meet me at the tasting room until the afternoon, so any investigating I did in the morning would have to have been done on my own, or with just Todd. I wasn't interested in spending a bunch of alone time with Todd, and I figured it was better to wait until we could all get together, anyway.

I closed down the pie shop as quickly as I could that afternoon, not even bothering to finish cleaning up all the dishes. I figured I'd come back later or come in extra early in the morning. That wasn't my usual style, but I just couldn't wait to get down to the winery and start investigating. I knew it wasn't likely that one of the tasting room employees would jump out as the guilty party who'd been helping to steal money from the city and kill off Caitlin, but a girl could hope, right? Maybe there would at least be a clue that would point me in the right direction.

When I got to the winery, I left Sprinkles outside in the shade with a pile of dog treats and his favorite chew toy. He gave me a wounded look, but I shook my head at him.

"You know I'd bring you in if I could, but it's against the rules. Bark if you need anything, but you should be busy for a while with those treats."

When I went inside, Todd was already there. He was sitting at the far right side of the tasting room with several small wine glasses in front of him. It looked like he'd already had a full tasting, because all but one of the glasses was empty. I rushed over to him.

"Hey, I hope you haven't been waiting long," I said, and then gestured to his tasting glasses. "Why didn't you just order a full glass?"

Todd shrugged. "I've been here about an hour. I don't have much to do in this town other than investigate Caitlin's murder, so I decided to come on down here and see if I could get a head start on observing the staff. But all I've observed so far is that they're jerks who let some customers order wine by the glass and not others."

As he spoke, he gestured toward the other end of the bar. I followed his gaze, and saw to my surprise that Violet and Grams were sitting on the other end of the bar, both with large, full glasses of wine in front of them. My eyes widened. I had been so focused on Todd when I walked in that I hadn't seen them. They must not have seen me, either. Their backs were turned toward me, and they looked like they were lost in some sort of deep discussion.

"Oh, don't take it personally. That's Violet, and she practically owns a barstool here. The employees make an exception for her, but only her. And that other woman is actually my grandma. I don't know what she's doing here, but I better go say hello. I'll be right back."

Todd made a face. "Your grandma hangs out with the crazy old lady who ran into Caitlin's body after she fell over dead in the street?"

"Yeah," I admitted. "Violet's not my favorite person either, but Grams is forcing me to be nice to her. She says it's been hard on the old woman to go through this whole ordeal, and that it's making her anxiety act up. Don't worry, I'll be right back. I just have to say hello. If I don't, Grams will bring Violet over here to say hello. Would you rather that?"

Todd made another face. "I guess not. But hurry. I'm anxious to start working on this murder case."

"I'll be quick," I promised, and then made my way down to the other end of the room.

As I approached Grams and Violet, Grams' face lit up. Violet gave me a nasty glare, but I smiled sweetly at her just to irritate her.

"Izzy!" Grams said. "What a pleasant surprise. I didn't even see you walk in. Why don't you pull up a stool and join us? I had no idea you were coming out today."

She glanced at her watch, a slight look of concern creasing her features. "As a matter fact, shouldn't you still be at the pie shop?"

"I closed a bit early today. I had plans to meet friends here, and the last hour at the pie shop is usually pretty slow anyway."

The scowl on Violet's face deepened. "You're meeting friends here? Is that Todd guy your friend?"

Violet and Grams both looked over at Todd, and I glanced back at him as well. He gave a small wave when he saw us looking at him, and Grams and I both waved back. Violet did not.

"Why are you associating with the likes of him?" Violet hissed. Then she turned to Grams. "I swear, Agnes. You know I love you dearly, and we've been through thick and thin together. I don't mean to question your granddaughter's senses, but you must admit that that young man isn't the best choice of company. He's likely in on Caitlin's murder, even if he himself didn't actually put the poison in Caitlin's drink." She turned to look at me. "Izzy, really. You shouldn't be associating with him. He's dangerous and has bad morals."

I looked at Grams for support, but she only shrugged at me as if to say "What can you do? Violet is Violet, and she's always a little crazy."

So I turned to Violet myself. I would have really gone off on her if Grams hadn't been there. But Grams' earlier admonitions to take it easy on Violet were still ringing in my ears, so I restrained myself as much as I could.

"Thank you for your concern, but I'll associate with whomever I choose. Besides, haven't you heard? Theo has been arrested. Mitch himself made the arrest, and Theo has been charged with the murder. I highly doubt that Todd was colluding with Theo, so if it's true that Theo committed the murder, then Todd is probably innocent." I crossed my arms over my chest defiantly.

Violet's face paled, which surprised me. Had she really not heard about Theo's arrest yet? It had been the hottest gossip in town today. But from Violet's reaction, it was almost as though she hadn't known.

When she did speak, however, she was nodding her head slowly. Her hands and her voice both shook. "I know. I heard. And it's the most ridiculous thing I've ever heard! There's no way Theo committed that murder. Didn't anyone listen to me when I said I saw Josie putting something in Caitlin's drink? It's like no one cares about real evidence anymore! Besides, if Theo did do something wrong, it's only because he was heartbroken over his mother's death, and didn't have a good womanly influence in his life. His father did not raise him to be a thief, and he especially didn't raise him to be a murderer. My guess is that Josie and Todd worked together to kill Caitlin, and now they're trying to pass the blame off on Theo."

I said nothing as Violet ranted, which seemed to irritate her. She continued ranting in an even higher-pitched voice.

"Such a sad state of things! If Mitch would only believe me, and see the truth of things, then Theo wouldn't have been arrested. Why would someone crunch up a pill and put it in someone's drink behind their back like Josie did, unless they were doing something wrong? This whole thing is a setup, I tell you! Josie and Todd are just trying to get away with murder!"

Violet's shaking was growing worse with every passing second, and Grams was giving me a warning look. I resisted the urge to roll my eyes, and instead made my way back to my seat without another word to Violet. I wanted to give Grams an earful about how she wasn't really helping Violet by letting the woman continue to avoid the truth of the matter. Theo had been arrested, and while I didn't think he was guilty, I didn't think that shouting about Josie and Todd was going to help things much. Violet should take her own advice to me and stay out of this investigation altogether.

Todd raised an eyebrow as I once again sat down beside him. "What was that all about?"

I shook my head. "Nothing exciting. Just Violet being her usual crazy self. She gets on my nerves so much, but my grandma is friends with her and forces me to be nice to her."

Todd chewed on his lower lip and looked over at Violet. I wondered what he was thinking. I wondered if it was possible that Josie had poisoned Caitlin's drink after all. Sure, she hadn't had any poison in that pill bottle I stole from her. But as far as I knew Mitch hadn't completed a search of her hotel room yet. What if there was poison in there? What if she'd had poison on her, but had gotten rid of it all because she knew she might be searched? Could I still completely discount the Josie theory? Maybe, for the time being, I should tell Mitch that I wanted to press charges against her, just so that she'd be forced to stay in jail. All of the suspicion seemed to have been taken off of her now that Theo had been accused. But if Theo *was* innocent, I couldn't completely write off the possibility that Josie might still be guilty.

I didn't exactly want to voice all of this to Todd. He was convinced of Josie's innocence, and all I would do by implying that Josie might be guilty was make Todd angry. I didn't want to make Todd angry right now, so I kept my mouth shut. I needed his help. He might have clues in his photographs still, or he might be able to see something in the tasting room employees that I would miss. I decided for the moment to keep the focus on Violet and her craziness, and not mention Josie.

"I guess I can't be too hard on her for being psycho," I said with a laugh. "After all, she was spurned by love. She dated Theo's dad, you know. But Theo's dad probably saw right through her craziness and knew she just wanted his money."

I expected Todd to laugh at this as well. But instead, he frowned. "Well, I'm not pretending to be an expert on the families in Sunshine Springs. But I don't think Violet was after old Mr. Russo for his money. I heard that Violet is from one of the wealthiest families in town. Apparently, she was heiress to a large fortune."

"Well, she was. *Was* being the operative word here. Grams told me that her family lost their fortune, and that's a big part of where all her anxiety issues come from. She went from being wealthy and not having a care in the world to having to worry about how to keep the electricity on in her house."

Todd's frown deepened. "She must not have lost everything. Look how well-dressed she is."

I looked over at Violet. She wasn't dressed as flashily as Grams. Violet wore a simple black dress as she often did, but her dress did look like it was made of a high quality material. Her shoes looked like they were real leather, and she also had diamond studs in her ears. The earrings matched a diamond-studded gold necklace around her neck. But the jewelry could have been fake, and since she wore pretty much the same thing all the time, she might just have one or two high quality black dresses that she rotated through.

I shrugged, and looked back at Todd. "She *is* dressed nicely. Maybe she's getting back on her feet a bit. But I don't think she has much. She probably only has a few nice outfits, you know?"

"Yeah, a few nice outfits that cost more than my monthly rent in San Francisco. Look at this. I was looking through photographs before you got here, and Violet is in quite a few of the ones I took the day Caitlin was murdered."

Todd pulled his laptop out of his messenger bag and set it in front of me. As the screen came to life, I saw that he'd been looking through thumbnails of his photographs. He furrowed his brow and scrolled for a moment until he found what he was looking for.

"Aha! There!" He double clicked on the thumbnail to open a photo. The photo showed Violet in her usual barstool at the tasting room, with her usual large glass of wine. She was wearing a black dress, but a different one from the one she was wearing today—and her jewelry was different as well. Still diamonds and gold, but a different design.

I frowned. "I guess she does have a few nice outfits. But saying they're worth more than your monthly rent is probably a bit of a stretch."

"Are you serious? Look at her bag in that photo."

I squinted at the bag, but it didn't mean anything to me. "And?"

Todd widened his eyes at me. "Are you serious? You don't recognize that bag? It's a Louis Vuitton, and it's huge. That thing must have cost a fortune. And look at the bag she has right now."

I glanced over and took a peek at Violet's bag. But aside from looking as though it was made of nice leather, nothing about the sleek black tote stood out to me. I shrugged my shoulders helplessly.

"Sorry, I guess I'm not up on the latest handbag designers. I spend half my life covered in flour, so it doesn't make much sense for me to spend money on an expensive purse that's only going to get ruined. And when I worked as a lawyer I saved every last penny for my dream of opening a pie shop."

Todd gave me an exasperated, long-suffering look. "That bag over there is a Hermes—more expensive even then a Louis Vuitton. Don't tell me that woman has no money. Maybe she's playing up the fact that her family lost their business to get sympathy, but if she's really having trouble paying for her electricity, all she has to do is sell one of those bags. She'll have enough money to pay her electric bill for the entire year, if not more. She's just trying to milk her past misfortunes for all they're worth. I also don't think her nervous shaking is as bad as she makes it out to be, because it doesn't happen all the time. I'm not saying she doesn't have anxious tendencies, but I think she overplays them quite a bit."

I glanced over at Violet again, taking in her expensive handbag, pricey dress, and glistening diamonds. Todd was right. Her shaking wasn't as constant as I'd thought it was. Even though she'd been shaking violently when I walked away from her and Grams, she wasn't shaking at all at the moment. Her hand looked quite steady as she lifted her wine glass and laughed at something Grams had said.

I frowned. "You're right. She isn't shaking at all right now. That's weird."

And then, suddenly, everything clicked for me. A horrible, sickening feeling rose in my stomach, and I swayed a bit in the barstool.

"Oh my gosh," I said. "How could I have not seen this before?"

"Seen what?" Todd asked. "Hey, are you all right? You look quite pale."

Just then, Scott and Molly arrived. As they walked up to Todd and me, they also must have been struck by the pale color of my face.

"Izzy?" Molly asked, reaching out a hand to steady me. "Are you alright?"

I jumped down from the barstool. "I'm fine. Will one of you please call Mitch and tell him to get over here right away?"

Scott pulled out his cell phone, but paused. "Okay. But why?"

"Just do it!" I said. "And tell him to hurry!"

I started walking away from the barstool.

"Wait!" Molly said. "Where are you going? What are you doing?"

"I'm doing something I should have done a long time ago. I'm going to have a little chat with Violet."

Chapter Twenty-Three

Ignoring the confused questions that Scott, Molly and Todd continued to throw my way, I marched over to where Violet was sitting and pointed my finger straight into her face.

"It was you! All this time, you've been playing the victim and acting like this whole ordeal has been so hard on you. You've been pointing fingers at Josie and Todd because it gave you a convenient someone to blame. I'll bet you're even happy about Theo being falsely arrested, even though you feel guilty at the trouble you're causing for old Mr. Russo's son."

Predictably, Violet immediately started shaking. "Agnes! Contain your granddaughter! What is this madness she's attacking me with?"

Grams gave me a sharp look. "Izzy? What's going on here?"

"What's going on is that I've finally solved this murder like you thought I could. Violet did it. She's been stealing money from the city for who knows how long. When she thought she'd get caught, she panicked and took Caitlin out."

"I would never!" Violet exclaimed. "Sunshine Springs is my home. It has been my home for my entire life. And I don't appreciate some outsider like you coming in and accusing me of such horrible crimes!"

"Then you shouldn't have committed those crimes," I said.

In the distance, I heard the sound of police sirens. Violet heard them too, and looked toward the door with unmistakable panic in her eyes.

"You're wasting your time, child," she said. "All you're doing is making a fool of yourself. Do you think anyone will accept you in

Sunshine Springs as a local after you falsely accuse me? I've been here decades longer than you've even been alive."

"Then you should be older and wiser than your actions indicate," I told her. "Did you really think that no one would notice your expensive clothing, jewelry, bags and car? Did you really think you could steal money from the city, spend it on such extravagant items, and not get caught?"

"I have a few nice things, yes," Violet said. "They're left over from the time when my family actually had money. I've had a very hard life, as everyone in Sunshine Springs knows. No one else begrudges me a few luxury items here and there."

From the corner of my eye, I saw Grams frowning in Violet's direction. "But Violet, dear, you were just complaining to me that you don't know how to pay your electric bill. Are you telling me those diamonds are real? I'd always assumed they were fakes, since you talk about money like you have none. But surely if you don't have money for electricity and food, you could sell some jewelry to pay for it."

"These are family heirlooms! I can't be expected to sell them away!"

I scoffed. "I highly doubt they're family heirlooms. The truth is that you couldn't stand the fact that you're no longer wealthy. After your family lost their business, you stewed about it for years. Decades, even. At one point, you must have thought that marrying the elder Mr. Russo was the answer to your troubles. You went after him hard, thinking that if he married you, you'd be set for life once again. But he proved to be harder to catch than you thought."

"You hush your mouth!" Violet said. Her face was turning a shade of purple that closely matched her name. "I wasn't after old Mr. Russo for his money. I loved him!"

"Oh, I'll give you that," I said. "I think you really did fall in love with him. It may have all started as a scheme to get his money, but I think you did develop a soft spot for him. That's why you always talk about him with such glowing praise. And I think it's why you felt it was your duty to defend Theo when the murder first happened. But at the end of it all, no matter how much you may have cared for Mr. Russo, your love for him still wasn't enough to make you admit to the murder to keep Theo safe. That's why Theo is still in jail right now, while you're walking free."

At that moment, Mitch burst into the tasting room with a couple of his officers on his heels.

"What's going on in here?" he asked, his sharp eyes scanning back and forth across the room. "I got a call from dispatch that someone here called the station and said they'd caught Caitlin's murderer."

I raised my arm. "That's right. Your murderer is right over here." I pointed at Violet.

Mitch looked at me like I was crazy.

"Violet?" he finally managed to choke out.

I could see the doubt in his eyes. He was beginning to think that I was crazy, and that he'd come down here for nothing. I supposed that everyone in town would think that at first, but they would learn the truth soon enough. I nodded in Mitch's direction.

"Yes, Violet. Get a warrant to search her home. I'm sure you'll find that she has records of emails about the money stolen from the city. Oh, it might all be encrypted on a laptop or something, but I promise you it's there. She couldn't stand not having money, so after her attempts at winning over a rich husband failed, she began scheming other ways to get it. I don't know who exactly on the City Council has been helping her, but she managed to convince someone there to pilfer money from the city and give it to her. I would imagine that whoever it is was getting a generous cut of that money."

"This is all lies!" Violet shouted.

I ignored her and continued. "It was easy enough for Violet to hide the money. She complained so loudly about her poor state of things that everyone believed her. And people here in Sunshine Springs probably don't pay much attention to fashion brands, so they didn't realize how expensive her purses and clothing are. By not being too flashy, she got away with things. Adding in the fake nervous shaking was a nice touch."

"What are you talking about?" Violet demanded. "You think I enjoy this anxiety that plagues me? You think it's all an act? Agnes! Silence your granddaughter! She's making a fool of herself."

Grams raised an eyebrow at Violet. "Actually, I'm inclined to let Izzy speak. Especially since there seems to be some truth in what she's saying."

"Truth?" Violet spat out. "There's no truth in what she's saying! You've known me for years! You know that none of this is an act."

"Do I?" Grams asked mildly. "Because it seems a little strange to me that you're not shaking right now. I can hardly think of anything that would be more stressful than this moment, but you're steady as an arrow right now."

Grams nodded at Violet's hand, which was still holding her wine glass. The wine in the glass was almost completely still. Violet wasn't shaking at all. I looked over at Mitch, and saw that his suspicion was starting to grow.

"Violet?" he asked with a crack of his knuckles. "Do you want to explain all of this?"

"There's nothing to explain!" she insisted.

"Yes there is," I said. "Violet's been stealing money, and she's been faking anxiety and poverty to get away with it. But then Caitlin somehow got wind of a possible scandal. Of course, everyone thought it was the winery stealing money. But even though the investigation wasn't aimed at Violet in the beginning, she still got nervous. She decided, like her little City Council friend suggested, that the best thing to do was to take out Caitlin. She poisoned Caitlin, thinking she could easily blame Josie and Todd since they argued with Caitlin so much. She made up that story about Josie putting pills in Caitlin's drink. She even went so far as to run over Caitlin when Caitlin collapsed in the street from the poison. She must have been quite happy when Caitlin fell right in front of her. She could make doubly sure the girl was dead, and no one would suspect her. After all, who would point fingers at a little old lady who'd been here in town forever?"

"But how did she poison Caitlin?" Todd asked, breaking into the conversation. "Don't get me wrong. What you're saying makes sense, and she is acting awfully guilty. But I was with Caitlin all day the day she died. Sure, I saw Violet around both here and at the Drunken Pie Café. But I never saw her get close enough to where she could have snuck something into Caitlin's drink."

I raised an eyebrow at Todd. "Oh, she didn't have to sneak anything into Caitlin's drink. She just had to make sure Caitlin drank from a special, poisoned bottle of wine. A bottle of wine that I'm sure is still sitting on the shelves back there somewhere. Let me ask you this, Todd. Did any of the employees here ever offer Caitlin a glass of the *special* 2016 reserve?"

Todd furrowed his brow. "Come to think of it, one of them did offer the special reserve to Caitlin at one point. She tried to wave it away by saying she'd had enough wine, but he insisted. He said it was the best wine here, and that if she was going to write a report on the winery then she absolutely had to try it."

I nodded, and looked back at the tasting room employees. "So," I asked. "Which one of you is getting paid off by Violet to serve a *special* 2016 reserve whenever she requests it?"

I thought I saw one of the employees go pale, but before any of them could speak, Violet lost it.

"You horrible, horrible child! I can't believe that you would go after a poor old woman like me! All I was trying to do was live the life of comfort that I deserved—the life of comfort I would have had if I hadn't unfairly lost my fortune to my father's idiocy! Everything was going fine. Even after Caitlin came, everything was going fine. I would have easily eliminated her and that would've been the end of it. But no! You had to come in and start nosing around. No matter how much I tried to throw blame on other people, you couldn't leave it alone, could you?"

Violet's face was definitely a hue of purple by this point. I glanced back at Mitch and saw his mouth hanging open. All around the tasting room, everyone else was staring at the drama unfolding— the employees, Scott, Molly, Todd, and Grams. Not to mention all of the tourists, who were getting quite a bit more than they'd bargained for when they came to the Sunshine Springs winery for a tasting.

Mitch started to step forward, motioning to his officers to follow him. I saw him reach to grab the pair of handcuffs hanging from his belt. Violet saw it too, and started screaming at me again.

"I should have given you the special reserve, too! The only reason I didn't was I thought your grandmother would keep you in line, but I guess she's not as loyal as I thought she was! I should have taken you out when I had the chance!"

The next thing I knew, Grams' fist was connecting with Violet's face, and Violet was tumbling off her barstool onto the ground. Grams hopped down from her own stool and stood over Violet.

"You listen to me," Grams yelled as she shook her fist above Violet's face. "Don't you dare accost my granddaughter! I *am* loyal— loyal to her. I push her hard, yes. I want her to be a strong woman and take care of things herself, because she's very capable, as you've seen. But if you think for one moment that I wouldn't step in to protect her with my very life if she was truly in danger, then you've really learned nothing about me over the last several decades."

Now *my* jaw hung open in shock. "Grams! You stood up for me."

Grams stood tall and brushed some imaginary dust off of her highlighter yellow blouse. "Of course I did, Izzy. I'll always stand up for you when it really counts."

Violet sputtered, but she didn't have a chance to get another word in before Mitch was pulling her up and reaching to put her hands behind her back. "Violet Murphy, you're under arrest for the murder of Caitlin Dixon. You have the right to remain silent. Anything you say can and will be used against you in a court of law…"

I saw a flash of movement out of the corner of my eye. Molly was digging in her purse to pull out her phone. As Mitch started to lead Violet out of the tasting room, Molly held up her phone and took a selfie with Violet and the police officers in the background. I shook my head as I walked over to her.

"Really?" I asked. "A selfie of a murderer being arrested?"

Molly grinned. "What can I say? I can't pass up an opportunity like that. Think of all the likes and comments I'll get for that one!"

I started to laugh, but my laugh was cut off by an unexpected hug from Todd. When he pulled back, he looked a little bit embarrassed, and his eyes might have been tearing up.

"Thank you so much, Izzy. I'm sorry for all the times I wasn't exactly nice to you in this process."

I shrugged. "I'm sorry if I wasn't nice at times, too. Trust me: I understand the stress you've been going through. I'm just happy that the real perpetrator has been caught, and I'm looking forward to getting on with my life now."

Todd smiled. "Me too. I can't wait to go back to San Francisco without feeling like a fugitive."

I smiled. There had been a time in my life that I would have been eager to get back to San Francisco as well. But that time was over. My life was in Sunshine Springs now, and I had a feeling that after the events of today, I had cemented my standing as a local in the community.

And what a community it was. Scott was reaching over to put an arm around me to make sure I was okay. Grams was shaking her head, muttering how she couldn't believe that Violet had had her fooled. And Molly was scrolling through her phone to her social media accounts to post her selfie. I knew that within minutes, the gossip train in Sunshine Springs would be running full speed.

But this time, I would be the hero on the gossip train, and not the villain.

Chapter Twenty-Four

The next day, the line in the Drunken Pie Café was out the front door. Everyone in town was once again stopping by to see whether I could expound on the local gossip. I had been a little bit afraid that people would be angry over the fact that I'd been responsible for putting Violet away. After all, I was still viewed as somewhat of an outsider, and Violet had been a local for decades.

But it turned out that I'd had nothing to worry about. Violet hadn't been very well liked in the community after all, but no one had wanted to admit it until she was accused of murder. And everyone was grateful that I'd gotten Theo out of prison. He was something of a local celebrity, and no one in Sunshine Springs wanted him behind bars.

The lines kept coming until I turned the sign in the window over to "Closed." It still took about an hour after that for me to finish serving everyone, but I wasn't about to kick anyone out. I was happy for the business, and I was happy to finally feel like part of the community. When at last my final customer had left, I started cleaning up. I was almost done when I heard a knock at the front door. I turned around and looked up, thinking I would send this person away. I didn't have much pie left to sell even if I'd wanted to. And at this point, I wasn't sure I wanted to. I was exhausted, and ready to go take a nice, long bath at home.

But when I looked up and saw the face outside the front door, it was Theo grinning back at me. I grinned myself, and then went to open the door for him.

He'd called me last night to say thank you, but I'd missed the call. I'd been quite exhausted by the time I'd gotten home from the winery. I had to admit, I'd been a little disappointed that I hadn't

153

seen Theo in the pie shop today. But I knew he probably wasn't ready to face the crowds yet, and I couldn't blame him for that.

Now that things were quiet, here he was. And he was looking much better than he had the last time I'd seen him. Gone were the dark circles under his eyes, and his formerly pale skin glowed with a healthy color once again.

"Hey," he said softly as I let him in and then locked the door behind him. "I heard that this is the best place in town to come both for pie and also for help if you've been accused of murder."

I grinned. "It's definitely the best place for pie. But don't go spreading the word that I help with murder cases. I made a special exception for you, but I'm really trying to phase out my lawyer career."

"Fine. Your secret's safe with me." Theo winked at me. "But I did want to come by and say thank you. I seriously don't know how I can thank you enough, but I at least had to tell you that I'm in your debt forever."

I blushed with pleasure, but waved him away. "It was nothing. I did what any decent person would have done when they thought someone had been falsely accused. Now, come on. You have to try this drunken pie I made. It's called death by chocolate, and it's a chocolate red wine pie made with your 2016 reserve."

Theo threw back his head and laughed. "Not a *special* 2016 reserve, I hope."

I grinned at him. "Nothing special about it, except that it tastes delicious."

I cut him an extra big slice of pie, and then poured two glasses of wine. I raised my glass to his and smiled. "Here's to not being thrown in jail for the rest of our lives for a murder we didn't commit."

"I'll toast to that." Theo clinked his glass with mine. Then he took a sip of his wine, followed by a bite of the pie.

"Oh gosh, this is delicious. How do you make it taste so good?"

I beamed, pleased at his praise. "I can't tell you, or I'd have to kill you."

Theo groaned. "Okay, enough with the murder jokes already. But seriously, this is an amazing pie. I don't think you're going to have any trouble getting this café off the ground. I'll definitely send business your way from the tasting room. After all, people need to eat a little something after a wine tasting. They might as well eat a boozy pie and continue the party."

I grinned. "Thanks. I really appreciate it. I'm feeling better about everything now, but for a few days there I was worried that I had wasted my life's savings on a pie shop that was never going to work out."

"I'd say your days of worrying are over. You're pretty much a hero in town. But more importantly, you helped clear the streets of Sunshine Springs of a very dangerous character. A couple of dangerous characters, actually."

"Oh? Did they figure out who was working with Violet?"

"Yup. They figured out a lot of things, actually. Once Mitch got Violet in the interrogation room, she sang like a bird. She agreed to tell him pretty much everything as long as he agreed to petition the judge on her behalf for a lighter sentence. Not that it matters much how many years she's sentenced to. She's so old that even a light murder sentence will probably have her behind bars for the rest of her life."

"I suppose so. Who did she implicate?"

"She told Mitch which City Councilman was helping her steal money. He was a treasurer, and he was giving Violet money in exchange for her continued support of him as a City Councilmember. Seems that at some point a few years ago, she found out he was stealing from the city. Instead of turning him in, she agreed to keep quiet as long as he would share the funds he stole with her."

"Sheesh. And then when they were almost caught they decided that murdering someone was better than owning up to stealing money?"

Theo nodded sadly. "I guess so. I'll never understand some people. Then again, I don't understand how someone could steal like that in the first place, so I *really* don't understand how someone could commit murder over the money. Poor Caitlin really got mixed up in a bad deal."

"How did Caitlin get mixed up in it, anyway? It seems odd that a reporter from San Francisco would have the emails and account records she did. How'd she get them?"

"One of the other City Councilmen suspected that something was going on. He did some investigating on his own, but couldn't find much. He brought it to the mayor, and the mayor couldn't find much either. They decided that if they put it in the hands of a journalist, that journalist might uncover clues they were missing. Of course, they never expected that things would turn out the way they did, and that the journalist would end up dead. Mitch was having a fit about all of it. You should've heard him ranting about how everyone wants to play detective instead of leaving the detective work to the real detectives."

I rolled my eyes. "Yeah he's given me a speech or two about that. But he can't be too mad at me. After all, I did solve the murder in the end."

"That you did. And you were right. It was the special 2016 reserve. Violet paid off one of the tasting room employees to have a special poisoned bottle of wine that he would serve to whomever she asked. He swears he didn't know it was actually poisoned. He says he thought it was just a laxative or something." Theo shrugged. "I guess I'll let the courts work that out. All I know is that he's definitely lost his job in the tasting room, and that bottle of special wine has been turned over to the police for evidence."

I frowned. "Do you think that's going to hurt your business?"

Theo laughed. "I was quite worried about it, but I have to say that if today's sales are any indication, the infamy of this whole murder case is actually going to help my business. You should've seen the tasting room. It was packed wall to wall."

I nodded. "Yeah, I bet. This has all been good for my pie shop as well."

I looked around for a few minutes as I sipped my wine, taking in the pristine café and the fact that it was all mine. Everything seemed to have worked out exactly the way I needed it to, but as Theo finished up his last bite of pie, I did have one more question for him.

"I've been meaning to ask you…remember when I saw you that day talking to the mayor and Mitch outside of the police station? What were you guys talking about? I have to admit I thought the meeting looked suspicious. But since you've been completely cleared and Violet has been implicated, I'm assuming the meeting wasn't anything shady."

Theo furrowed his brow for a moment, trying to remember. Then his face brightened. "Oh! That! We were planning a hundredth birthday party for Edgar Bates. He's the oldest citizen in Sunshine Springs, and he's turning one hundred next month. The mayor wants the winery to provide the drinks. He just happened to be at the station that day to talk to Mitch about something else, so he was asking me a few questions about the party. You should come to that party, by the way."

I smiled. "I'd love to."

Theo gazed at me intensely for a moment, then lowered his voice and said, "You should come as my date."

I blushed. "Listen, Theo. About that…I think I've realized that I need some time to heal. As you know, I just got divorced, and I'm not sure I'm ready for anything romantic quite yet. Although, if you don't mind, I would like to finish up the tour of your winery. We never did get to finish looking at the grapevines."

Theo smiled. "Okay. I'm not going to lie—I'm a little disappointed that you're not interested in a date. But I understand. Maybe in the future?"

The hopeful look in his eyes melted my heart. "Maybe. With any luck, I'll be staying in Sunshine Springs for a long, long time. And with any luck, things will quiet down a bit now. I moved to a small town because I thought life would move at a slower pace here."

Theo laughed. "I wouldn't count on things slowing down too much. You seem like the kind of person who attracts adventure."

I gave Theo a flirtatious wink, and then grabbed his fork from him. I scooped up the last bite of his pie and popped it into my mouth.

"You might be right," I said with a shrug and another wink. "We'll just have to wait and see."

About the Author

Diana DuMont lives and writes in Northern California. When she's not reading or dreaming up her latest mystery plot, she can usually be found hiking in the nearby redwood forests.

You can connect with Diana at www.dianadumont.com

Happy reading, and happy sleuthing!